Braced for Seduction

An Erotic Orthodontic Encounter

by
Catherine Aimes

An Intraoral Press publication

This is a work of fiction. All names, characters, incidents, events, and places are the product of the author's imagination. Any resemblance to actual persons, events, or places is entirely coincidental.

Copyright © Catherine Aimes 2017

ISBN: 978-1-387-23404-2

For additional information go to:
www.intraoralpress.com

e-mail: info@intraoralpress.com

A reminder:

Braced for Seduction is a work for more mature readers, involving sexual situations and stimulation.

Braced for Seduction is a work of fiction and for entertainment purposes some aspects of orthodontic treatment and wear might be exaggerated and the characters' experiences should not be considered representative.

Readers should not rely on any information or descriptions in these stories. For accurate information about orthodontic treatment readers are encouraged to consult a dentist or orthodontist, or to contact a professional organization such as the American Association of Orthodontists (www.braces.org).

*And just to make sure, an **additional** disclaimer*:

Braced for Seduction is a work of fantasy and fiction. It's not real. Parts are unrealistic. Attributes and behavior of the characters are exaggerated. Characters also act and react improperly and unwisely, and the depictions of this in the novel should *emphatically not* be equated with approval of it. Enjoy *Braced for Seduction* as fantasy. It's entertainment for the imagination, not imitation.

Contents

Friday 9
Saturday 21
Sunday 99
Epilogue 131

   About the author 137

Friday

1.

Mom was excited to see her college friend. They had always stayed in touch, and would meet at reunions and the rare times when they were in the same city, but it had been a couple of years since the last time. I had only met April Devere once, and only had a hazy memory of her. But Mom didn't need to remind me who she was, because she had one of the more exciting jobs I had ever heard of. She was a location scout for movies and TV shows.

That was what was bringing her to our part of the country. She had spent the week crisscrossing the state, looking for possible sites for a big project she was working on, and she was going to finish her regional tour in the towns close to where we lived, so Mom had convinced her to come visit. We could be home base for her as she scouted the last closest locations before she had to leave Sunday, to catch her flight back home. Mrs.Devere liked the idea and was happy to accept the invitation.

Mom warned me that Mrs.Devere was bringing her son, Charles, too. She had brought him along on her trip, combining work with a sort of end of season vacation getaway before school started in a couple of weeks. Giving them some mother-son time, and letting Charles experience first-hand what his mom did, well as giving him a chance to see parts of the country he'd never been to.

Mom hadn't met Charles, but she scrolled through the old emails from Mrs.Devere and found a Christmas card from two years ago which included some family pictures. He looked young there, but I had to admit that he was good-looking. Mom noticed too, and I could see her frown as she wondered how she was going to handle having two teens in the house.

Charles was also in high school, and apparently a year older than me. "He's starting eleventh grade, April said," Mom told me. "I think she said he was sixteen."

A year older, and a grade ahead of me.

2.

It was Mom that heard that car pull up on the gravel driveway and shouted, "They're here!" It was fun to see Mom get so excited about seeing an old friend.

We went to the door and I recognized Mrs.Devere right away. She was tall, tanned, and looked so sophisticated. Mom is a confident, successful professional, but you could immediately tell that Mrs.Devere is so much more metropolitan. It wasn't that Mom looked plain beside her, but you could tell which one of them had lived the quieter life.

I paid even closer attention when the passenger door opened and Charles got out. My first impression was good. He looked a lot more mature than he had in the Christmas photo, and he was taller than his mother now, with broad shoulders and a good physique. And he really was handsome. My cheeks already felt hot as I stared, and I worried that I would immediately stutter out something stupid when he said hello.

He glanced at me but politely waited next to his mom as she hugged mine and the two of them almost pulled each other over. He began to grin at the scene, and then smiled when his mother finally introduced him. "Laura, this is my son, Charles."

My jaw dropped. Thank God they were all looking at each other. I couldn't believe it. He had braces! So much for that first impression – the metalmouth completely ruined it. I almost choked at the sight. A real, serious set of braces. With elastics connecting top and bottom jaws on each side, to reinforce the look.

Of course there were still some kids with braces in my grade. I had friends who still had braces. But...they had braces. We didn't ostracize them or anything like that, but you couldn't help but feel they belonged in a sort of different category. At school, there were boys, girls, jocks, nerds, cheerleaders...and there were kids with braces.

And Charles was one of those kids. Even though he was older than I was.

I gulped as they finally turned to me and I was glad that Mrs.Devere *oohed* and *aahed* and fussed over me when Mom proudly introduced me to her, so that my awkward handshake and *Hi* to Charles wasn't what everyone was paying attention to but could be treated almost like an afterthought.

They got their luggage and Mom and I showed them to the guest bungalow. We can't really put up people there in the winter, but in the summer it is actually cozy. Mrs.Devere and Mom talked non-stop, like they wanted to catch up about everything in the first ten minutes. Charles seemed to be used to his mother's hyperactivity and he just followed her calmly without saying anything. Of course he probably wanted to keep those braces hidden too – I sure would have.

It took like a quarter of an hour before Mom could tear herself away and actually let them settle in, and we went back to the house to prepare dinner. It was great to see Mom in such a good mood. She really liked seeing her old friend again.

It was a beautiful summer evening, so we prepared dinner out on the deck. Charles came and helped set the table and everything, and his mom followed soon after him.

Of course Mom and Mrs.Devere couldn't stop talking over dinner. So much to catch up on! Mrs.Devere also told us some about her current trip, with Charles nodding in agreement or responding more or less monosyllabically when she turned to him to confirm what she was saying or trying to get his input. Having braces can quieten you – who wants to display those? – but he seemed pretty laid-back anyway. I got the impression he was enjoying the trip but maybe getting a little bit tired of his mother's constant company. Putting myself in his shoes, I agreed. A road trip with Mom would be fun, but the adventure might start wearing thin after a week....

Friday was usually movie night – Mom and I would stream something on TV – but she and Mrs.Devere still has do much to talk about that when we were finishing dinner that she nudged me and suggested Charles and I find something to watch by ourselves. Since she said it in front of Charles I couldn't really say no. Not that I minded too much – but I hoped he wasn't just into action films....

3.

We helped clear the table and then I showed Charles where the den with the widescreen TV was.

"Yeah, OK," he nodded. "I'll be back in a minute."

I sat down on the sofa and answered some of the texts that had accumulated on my phone. Some of my friends were out and I kind of envied them doing something more fun on a Friday evening. They knew I usually couldn't do Fridays but I could at least enjoy some of what they did vicariously.

I did a double-take when Charles came back in.

He had a *headgear* on!

That arch of wire around the front of his mouth, attached to a neckstrap.

I couldn't believe it.

A few of the kids at school have had headgear, but mostly that was like when we were in fifth or sixth grade. One of my friends did get headgear last year, and it was such a shock when she first showed us. We still tease her mercilessly when she puts it on at sleepovers. Headgear!

And Charles was even older!

I couldn't stop staring. I was like paralyzed with shock. I knew some kids our age still had to wear it – Allison said she was going to have to wear it probably for the rest of the year – but it was still so...incongruous. And that he'd come right out and let himself be seen wearing it. I guess orthodontists are serious about how much time you have to wear something like that – that's what Allison says when she explains why she sometimes wears it after school and before she goes to bed – but surely that's something you want to keep *really* private. Like not let people you've just met see.

Charles calmly walked over and sat down on the couch near me, as if nothing was out of ordinary. Even though he not only had braces, which was already pretty bad, but he had this *thing* strapped to his face.

I couldn't keep myself from blurting out, "You have headgear?" I realized even as I was saying it that it was the stupidest, rudest non-question I could say. I mean, obviously he had headgear. There was no point in asking whether he had it, other than to point out that he did.

Charles didn't give me too withering a look, and when he saw my almost panicked wide-eyed stare he lowered his eyes, like he wanted to see for himself. Except of course that I don't think you can really see the headgear when you have it on. Or only sort of, like your nose – it really doesn't come in your field of vision. But he pretended he had to see it to believe it, and after a second he shrugged and nodded, like he was saying, *I guess so.*

I was mortified turning my gaze to the blank TV screen, wondering how I could make this better. But, really, I couldn't.

He finally broke the silence. "So what are we watching?" I had gotten the impression at dinner, but wasn't totally sure, because he really hadn't said much then – but now I could really tell how he slurred and lisped his words noticeably. Maybe the headgear exacerbated that. Whatever – those braces were a real piece of work.

I bit my lip, just relieved to change the subject. I turned the TV on and started clicking through the menus. We had to go through a couple of options – he'd seen this, I'd seen that – before finding an episode of a TV show we both followed but hadn't seen yet.

I was grateful to avoid having to look at him the entire time.

I scrolled through the texts on my phone while the credits rolled on the TV. I was tempted to gossip with my friends – though they'd probably tease me about my Friday date if I revealed I was sitting next to a sixteen-year-old boy with braces and headgear. On the one hand, it would be hilarious to report that to them. On the other hand, it was just too incredibly embarrassing.

I got thirsty a few minutes into the show. "I'm getting something to drink," I told Charles, forced to look at him again and trying my hardest to pretend to be completely unfazed by what he was wearing. "Do you want something?"

He tapped the headgear's facebow where it connected to the interior facebow, between his lips. "It gets in the way," he explained. "Too much of a bother. I'm OK."

I was glad to be able to turn and walk away – embarrassed to have yet again drawn attention to what he was wearing. Talk about elephants in a room. On a face.

At least the show was good. We laughed a bit, but it was engrossing enough that we didn't really talk, beyond the occasional *I can't believe he did that!* at the really cool scenes. And I forced myself to keep my eyes glued to the screen and *not* turn and stare at Charles's headgear.

At some point Mom and Mrs.Devere came in – to check on us, the way parents like to do, pretending to be totally casual but so obviously nosy.

"Enjoying the show?" Mom asked. I could see her eyes get all wide when she saw the headgear too, but she totally pretended not to notice.

Charles and I both nodded.

Mrs.Devere looked satisfied too. "Well, I'm glad to see you're wearing your oral chastity belt, Charles," she said with a smile. "At least we don't have to worry about you two getting into any sort of trouble."

Even I wanted to melt in my seat when she said that. Why do adults think when a teen boy and girl are in a room together that their hormones have to be raging completely out of control? Other than the fact that it's usually true…. I mean, Charles's braces already precluded any possible romantic interest, right? She must have known that. And *chastity belt*…I cringed at the sound thought of the words, and all their sexual implications. How could she?

Mom laughed a bit too, but it was sort of forced, like she was embarrassed for us too. And I couldn't help but glance at Charles, and even though he had managed to stay calm and laid-back the whole time so far, his cheeks were now flushed red in obvious incredible embarrassment.

It was one of those moments where you just want to disappear – and I'm sure it was ten times worse for him.

Fortunately the moms didn't say anything else and we could just turn back to the TV and try to pretend nothing had happened.

Yeah, right.

4.

When the closing credits rolled I stretched and yawned. I was, in fact, tired but I figured making that clearer would keep Charles from asking whether we were going to watch another episode, or something else. But he didn't say anything.

Turning off the TV I finally looked at him again. At his headgear.

I had to ask.

"You don't mind the headgear?"

He looked at me intently before saying anything. Like he was weighing how to answer. He turned his body so he was facing me, and he leaned in a little bit closer. "You had braces, right?"

I blushed. Hard. I knew it wasn't anything to be embarrassed about but I guess I sort of was. No, absolutely I was. Yes, I had had braces – but that was a while ago, and I didn't care to be reminded of it. It was part of the past.

I couldn't help but nod slightly, acknowledging I had. I couldn't lie about it.

"And you got retainers, right?"

I nodded. I hated this. I never spoke about my braces or retainers. Obviously my friends had seen me with them, but now I kept them out of sight and out of mind. I didn't take my retainers on sleepovers. No one ever saw me in them. For all intents and purposes no one knew I still had retainers – and I didn't want to admit I did. But he was forcing me into it.

"So you still wear them at night, right?"

I shrugged. I couldn't bring myself to say I did. I mean, I did – but that was something kept under the cover of darkness, in the privacy of my room and bed.

"Tell you what," he said, with that weird slurring to his voice. "You put your retainers in, then I'll tell you anything you want to know about me and all this." He motioned to the facebow and around his mouth – but continued to keep his mouth more or less closed, so I couldn't really get much of a view of the braces.

It wasn't an in your face kind of challenge. More like one of fairness? Maybe he felt since he was so exposed, in all his orthodontic humiliation, it was only fair I meet him partway.

I shook my head. Too fast, too nervous. Making way too obvious that what he demanded was way more than I could handle.

He laughed, and shrugged, and turned aside. "I guess I should head to bed," he slurred. "See ya tomorrow morning."

I nodded. Kind of dumbfounded. Strip the headgear and braces away and he was really pretty hot and cool. But there was no overlooking the braces, layered on. And then the headgear, strapped on. It wasn't that much metal, in sum – but more than enough to reduce him from someone whose attentions you might really want to a walking embarrassment.

I looked at my phone again. I was tempted to answer some of the texts from my friends with some choice snippets describing my evening. But I didn't even want to admit I'd spent most of it sitting next to a boy in headgear.

I was still lost in catching up on the Friday evening gossip on my phone when Mom came in and let herself fall onto the couch beside me.

"You had an OK time with Charles, Caroline?" she asked.

I shrugged. "We watched TV. It was painless. He made himself scarce as soon as it was over. Painless."

"It was great seeing April again."

"She seems cool."

"We thought you might want to come with us in the morning, when she scouts nearby. We could drop you two off back home after lunch – if you don't mind spending the afternoon with Charles too much?"

Mom looked at me pleadingly, like she was asking a big sacrifice from me. "You could go to the mall or a movie or something if you like. Or have some of your friends over. Just…you know, I wouldn't want you to leave him in the house alone while you go off doing something. I know it's a Saturday…."

"It's fine, Mom. We can hang here."

"You can go to the mall…."

"Mom! You saw his braces! I cannot be seen with a guy with braces!"

"I'm sure he doesn't have to wear that headgear thing during the day…."

"Mom! Of course not. But he has braces – I'd be such a laughingstock if anyone saw us…."

"But he's like an older boy. He's not even bad-looking, when he has his mouth closed. Your friends wouldn't be impressed?"

I groaned. Mom isn't as bad as some of the other parents, but she can be a bit dense at times. "Mom! Braces! If he were like twelve and I could pretend like I were babysitting then maybe. But this way everybody would think he's like my boyfriend or something, and I'd never be able to live it down."

Mom seemed to understand. She must have remembered my own awkward and humiliating years in braces, after all – not that we ever mentioned them. "You know," she said, "April told me he actually had braces before. Like when he was eleven or so. But apparently he didn't wear his retainers and by the time they realized it was too late and they had to put braces on again. Can you imagine?" She looked appropriately shocked. To have to wear braces a *second* time…!

But there was more. "Originally," she said gloomily, "he was supposed to get them off by now, after like a year, but apparently the orthodontist doesn't trust him to wear the retainers or something like that. The risk is too great of everything relapsing again, so he has to have them for at least another year."

Mom looked stunned that such a fate could befall anyone. I couldn't imagine what that must feel like. To be sentenced to a year more in braces than the orthodontist originally said. But I did remember that when I had them, it didn't help much knowing they should come off at a certain point. Time seemed infinite and endless anyway, and while it obviously would have been worse to have them longer it wouldn't have been abruptly, shockingly worse – more like just a continuation of the same misery.

"Shows you how important it is to wear those retainers," Mom said, shaking her head.

She couldn't even bring herself to say *you* and *your* to me. I think that if she could have, she would have wiped all memory of my having had braces away. We all wanted to forget my braces years – and everything associated with them. Even though she knew that I still wore my retainers at night, it was like she didn't want to know. She never mentioned them. Of course, neither did I. The less said about them, the better.

As Mom got up she smiled at me. "You know when April told me she was bringing her sixteen-year-old son with her, I was a bit worried about what to do with the two of you. I mean, I trust you and everything, but with a sixteen-year-old boy in the house…"

Mom!" I groaned, rolling my eyes. Like any adolescent, it always made me uncomfortable when Mom hinted at things like lust and sex and all those feelings.

"I know, I know. But, Caroline, parents can't help think about things like that. So I was so relieved when he smiled and revealed that set of braces...."

She didn't even need to say it. We both knew. Everybody knew. Braces weren't even a turn-off. With braces, there wasn't even a switch to worry about. With braces, anything that even came close to being *sexual* was totally unthinkable.

"And the headgear...," she couldn't help but smile as she winced.

Of course, that was the finishing touch. Anyone you'd seen in headgear – well, you couldn't unimagine that.

5.

I got changed and went to bed, checking my phone one last time.

I kept my retainers in their case hidden in the drawer in my nightstand. That night, I couldn't bring myself to take them out. I always wore them – unless a friend slept over, or I was sleeping over somewhere, of course. And Charles's example and what Mom told me should have scared me into putting them in as fast as possible, but I just couldn't bring myself to do it. The thought of Charles in bed, smirking through his headgear, *knowing* that I was supposed to put my retainers in....

No, I just couldn't do it. I felt guilty, but it was just one night, I told myself.....

Saturday

1.

Mom woke me up to let me know breakfast was almost ready. "We want to head out early," she reminded me. "You still want to come along with, right?"

I nodded groggily.

I was curious about Mrs. Devere's job. She had told us a bit about it the previous evening, and scrolled through her iPad, showing us all the pictures she took and how she organized them.

Lying back, trying to wake up, I felt a pang of guilt again at not having worn my retainers. Not that I missed waking up with their bulk and taste in my mouth. But, yeah, I felt like I had cheated a bit. And, like Mom and my orthodontist and every other moralizing adult would have told me, I was just cheating myself.

Fortunately, nobody knew or cared, so I could keep my little guilt trip to myself.

Charles and his mother were already at the table when I sat down. Now without his headgear it struck me again that Charles was really good-looking. Until he opened his mouth to take another spoonful of cereal, revealing his braces.

He kept the elastics on even when he ate, and those really framed the whole braces look. But at least he didn't have those colored ligatures on the braces themselves. I couldn't exactly tell, but clearly everything was all-metal there.

Mom had tried to convince me that colored ligatures were fun when I had my braces, but even at that age – I was like twelve – I could hear the strain in her voice, trying to put a good spin on something she thought was hopelessly awful. But I tried to convince myself too – after all, braces were something so horrible, any way you could maybe dress them up better had to be an improvement. But after the first couple of times trying out bright colors – pink and orange and light blue – I realized I was just trying to fool myself and everybody else, and none of us were falling for it. Friends told me not to get the clear or white ones, because they got stained and discolored from food, but I still thought those were best and insisted on those for the rest of my treatment time.

Charles grinned as he caught me staring at his braces, and I blushed and shook myself, grabbing toast and juice and stuffing my mouth so I wouldn't have to say anything.

Once we started driving Charles had that *been there, done that* look of the bored teen, while Mom and Mrs.Devere couldn't stop gabbing up front. It was fine by me. I was kind of excited to ride along, and see what Mrs.Devere did.

It didn't turn out to be too exciting, but it was kind of fun for a while. You never really turn off those backroads when you live nearby, and we explored a few buildings that I'd never really paid attention to or noticed. And since she explained what she was looking for, Mrs.Devere also kind of made you look at the scenery and landscape differently than normally. I could see how after a week of this Charles would have grown tired of it, but for one morning it was interesting to me.

On the way back we stopped for lunch, grabbing some hamburgers at a place where you could sit outside. Mrs.Devere had some good movie stories, and told us some funny things she'd experienced on the job. I guess Charles had heard most of this before, and he didn't say much, but occasionally he'd add a clever comment. He wasn't snarky, and he didn't undermine or make fun of his mother, but made the stories even funnier or better, adding a detail or different perspective.

It was weird how in most ways he wasn't at all like a little kid, or even the boys my age. He behaved really maturely. But then there were the braces, and the way they dominated his looks and affected his speech. When he talked and ate I notice there was some pink plastic behind his lower teeth, like a retainer – maybe that was what caused him to slur his speech the way he did. Maybe he even had an acrylic plate on the top too – it was impossible for me to tell.

If it weren't for the braces I would have totally been…more curious about him. He would have really been a boy I would have wanted to hang out with, I think. His whole presence and demeanor, it really appealed to me. But there was no way of looking or getting past the braces. Really no way.

2.

Mom and Mrs.Devere dropped us off at home and took off again in the other direction. Mom gave me that *be good* look, but it wasn't even as stern or long as the one she'd give me if she was leaving me alone with my girlfriends.

"The deckchairs are comfortable," I suggested to Charles. "But if you want to watch TV or something, make yourself at home."

"OK," he said, shrugging noncommittally. "Just going to go brush my teeth first."

At least he wasn't like the braced kids at school who didn't brush after every meal. I always found that really gross, and even though I always hated excusing myself to brush mine when I had braces it was worse those times when I didn't have a toothbrush with me and couldn't.

I got my phone and iPad and made myself comfortable on the deck. Charles came back a few minutes later.

"No headgear?" I teased him.

He gave an exaggerated stunned look, then felt his cheeks and lips with one hand like he was feeling for the facebow. "Guess not," he said. So there was a bit of snark in him.

"Don't mind me, if you want to wear it. Getting in more hours is good, right?"

He shrugged. "At night is fine." He sat down and turned on his iPad.

"You wore it while we watched TV yesterday," I pointed out.

He shrugged. "Made the moms feel more comfortable, right? Willing to leave us alone. Otherwise maybe Mom would have dragged me along all day today again. You know – boy, girl, empty house." He pointed first at himself, then me, then the house.

I laughed. I would have laughed normally too, because it was true. *Boy, girl, house, alone* was definitely a combination parents worried about. But *braced* boy? I had to laugh. That didn't even count....

"You didn't mind wearing it around...us?" I meant *me*, of course.

Another shrug.

"Your friends don't...say stuff?"

"I don't wear it around them. But here? You? Thousands of miles away from home? It's not like I'd see you at school next week." He finally put the iPad down and turned to me. Smiling, he said, "Much easier to be a little more daring. Take some risks."

Wearing headgear was a strange kind of daring, I thought. But since the braces barred pretty much any intimate ideas, why not go to the other extreme?

"Did you have it, when you had braces?"

I shook my head.

He turned back to his iPad. "You missed something."

Which seemed odd too. I mean, I sometimes wondered what it was like to have something like that. But obviously I was incredibly relieved never to have to be sentenced to wearing headgear by my orthodontist.

"You don't mind having the braces? Like at your age? I mean with girls and everything?" I blushed a bit, embarrassed by what I was saying but also curious.

"It's not a problem," he said coolly, looking at me with a bit of a smile.

"You're just willing to wait with dating and going out and stuff until they're off?"

He squinted a bit. "No," he said, drawing out the word, like I was on the wrong track. "I mean, sure, no one wants to be the girlfriend of a kid with braces, especially in high school. But girls are curious. You'd be surprised how many are curious what it feels like to make out with someone who has braces."

I jerked in my seat. I was surprised by the idea. "Come on," I said, like I was sure he was pulling my leg.

He smiled, and leaned closer to me. "Aren't you curious what it feels like?"

I flinched and pulled back, shocked by the idea and instinctively avoiding what I thought was going to be an attempt to kiss me.

He laughed and pulled back, leaning back in his chair, pleased with himself with the shock and scare he'd put in me. "Think about it. The contrast of the soft lips and tongue, and the hard metal edges of the braces. Girls can make out with normal boys anytime. And that mouthfeel is always the same. Braces – that's something different. Special. Almost unique. That opportunity doesn't come along often."

I shuddered and blushed. But no one would want that, would they? Even as I had to admit I was curious too. Even as I caught myself staring at his braces.

He looked back at me, arching his eyebrows, like he was asking, *Well?*

I shuddered again. I almost laughed at how absurd the idea was.

"Mom said you already had braces when you were younger," I tried to change the subject. Not getting very far. "And that you got them again now."

"Tell you what," he said, still leaning back and holding his face into the sun. "You put your retainers in, and I'll tell you anything you want to know. I'll tell you all about my orthodontic experiences."

"Thanks, no!"

"Suit yourself," he shrugged, without looking at me. "But think of this as the unique experience that it is. I mean, there are probably kids in your class with braces too, but you'll see them in class every day all year, so I get why you wouldn't want them to see you with your retainers, or talk to them about their braces. But me, I'm here one day, out of your life the next. Take advantage of the situation. Take some risks."

"Sounds like you're the one trying to take advantage. Pressuring me into embarrassing myself with my retainers."

"The choice is yours. It seems like a fair trade off to me. I've already shown you mine – all mine, right? Headgear and all. And I can't unshow you mine. And I can't escape from mine – the braces are securely cemented in place. So it's only fair for you to even the playing field. If you're embarrassed by your retainers, that's on you. I can't help how you feel about them."

I was almost stewing. Not even Mom asked me to put in my retainers. No one was even supposed to know I had retainers. Or at least they weren't supposed to acknowledge them. It was like my period, something to be handled quietly, discreetly, and totally personally.

And he didn't even seem to see how outrageous his demand was. He was looking at his iPad again, as if the conversation were over. He didn't even care whether or not I wore my retainers, he was just toying with me.

3.

"Want some soda?" I asked. I was thirsty and annoyed and couldn't concentrate on what I was reading.

"Great, yeah." He turned to me, "But nothing sugary, right?" he said, tapping his braces.

"Got it," I said, jumping up to keep myself from staring at that tangle of silvery metal in his mouth. He seemed to be fully with the orthodontic program: no sweets, brushing after meals, wearing his headgear. I remembered how annoyed I had been by some of the prohibitions, and hadn't been nearly as strict. And had two cavities to show for it.

I got some sodas from the kitchen, but walking back I stopped and went back to my room. I stood there for a moment, not believing it myself. *Am I really doing this?* I asked myself. But I was feeling reckless. Challenged. Annoyed by Charles's smugness. I opened the drawer to my nightstand and fished out the container in which my retainers clacked. I looked at it for a moment. *Am I really doing this?* I asked myself again.

I was.

I didn't take the retainers out. I didn't go that far. But I took the plastic case and went back out on the deck.

Charles looked up as I handed him the soda. "Thanks."

Then I demonstratively put down the small round case on the low table by our chairs. I wanted to look daringly at him, but I couldn't. Now that the existence of my retainers was literally out in the open I suddenly felt a whole lot less self-confident.

Seeing them he sat up and smiled. "Your retainers?" he grinned. Revealing that full-metal set of braced teeth.

I tilted my head and gave him a *Duh* look. I kept myself from saying something really stupid like, *No, it's a radio*.

He sat up and leaned forward even further. "Well, let's see them!" he said eagerly.

Now I really thought this had been a bad idea. That he'd back down. Who would want to see someone's retainers, much less humiliate them by making them put them in?

"Come on, you don't really want to see them," I said.

"Put them in!" he grinned.

"Come on, I can't even speak properly with them in."

"What about me?" he reminded me with his slurred speech. Opening his mouth a bit further he tapped the roof of his mouth with his index fingernail – except it wasn't the roof of his mouth. He did have like a retainer there too. "I have this huge plate wired in," he said. "Top and bottom."

"But mine are so big," I protested weakly. They weren't that big. It just felt that way. And something about my mouth or the way I talked meant they inhibited my speech more than bigger retainers did for some of my classmates.

"Let me see, at least," he said.

I tried to remember whether I had really cleaned the retainers last time I had put them in the case. It would be gross if they were covered with my dried out spit. Grosser – retainers were gross anyway.

I felt like I couldn't just take the closed container and walk away again. I couldn't totally back down. But I had never really *shown* my retainers to anyone. My parents, when I got them, but that was it. My friends only saw them in my mouth or not at all.

Reluctantly I opened the case and pulled out the two Hawley retainers. They were purple. For some reason, I hadn't wanted them to be the normal translucent pink, and I asked for purple. I hadn't wanted any designs on them – designs suggested the retainers were something to look at, and I didn't want anyone looking at mine. Not then, not now.

But Charles stared, smiling. "Those aren't so bad," he said.

I held up the top one to prove him wrong. It was a full-palate retainer. The acrylic layer wasn't too thick, but it covered most of my palate so it extended pretty far. It looked kind of big. It certainly felt dominating when I wore it.

"So put them in!" Charles encouraged me.

"I really can't talk with them...."

"Come on, you must have worn them fulltime for a few months, right?"

Three or four. And every time I spoke in class or had to read something aloud I could hear the tittering of my classmates at the way I sounded. Wearing them in public had been more agonizing than having braces.

"Come on, let's see what you look like with them," Charles prodded.

I knew what I looked like with them. Silly. Childish. Pathetic. Of course, looking at Charles staring so expectantly I could see the mouthful of braces he faced the world with, and that was obviously a whole another degree – or ten – of humiliation.

"You don't really want to…," I said.

"I do!"

Part of me felt it would somehow be only fair for the braced Charles to see me. Part of me kind of wanted to put them in in front of someone. Someone I was never going to see again, where it didn't matter what they thought. To reveal myself to them with my retainers, which were, after all, still such a big part of my life – worn every night – but such a hidden one.

I would never have considered putting them in in front of a *normal* boy. One who didn't have braces. One I would see again, like at school. That would have been too humiliating. But Charles had braces, so it wasn't like there could be any spark between us, or anything physical, and he was leaving the next day.

So, even as I barely knew what was possessing me I clicked the one retainer against the roof of my mouth, and the other over my lower teeth. I gave Charles a quick *There* smile, revealing the two wires now running across my top and bottom teeth – and I immediately felt on my tongue how much surface area the retainers really covered, taking over my mouth.

"There you go," Charles said. "They look great!"

I rolled my eyes. "Come on…," I slurred.

Charles looked more seriously again. "No, really. I don't get why girls don't see that more often. That it's pretty. The sleek silver wire straight across the teeth. That's beautiful! The other kind of retainers, those clear plastic covers, those are gross. But the silver wire – it's like jewelry. Like simple silver earrings. Elegant even."

I blushed. He sounded sincere, but it was so silly to think that anyone could find the look attractive. I mean maybe, in a way, but that was completely overwhelmed by the fact that what they yelled loud and clear was that you were wearing a retainer. After I didn't have to wear mine fulltime anymore I was supposed to put them in after dinner already, but Mom was like relieved to overlook that I 'forgot' to do that, and only put them in when I went to bed. She was like so relieved to see me not wearing them. Not looking like this.

"The way I sound when I wear them makes up for that," I suggested, my words coming out even more slurred and heavy than his.

He laughed.

I reached up to take the retainers out. Enough was enough. But Charles reached out and put his hand on my arm.

"Don't," he said, his tone a mixture of alarm and disappointment. It was so heartfelt it actually got to me. And his touch – I felt it. It was gentle but a real reaching out, too. Boys didn't touch me like that. I couldn't remember one ever having done so. A tiny, pleasant shiver went through me.

So I stopped, and swallowed – reminding me of the huge, obstructing retainers again – and waited.

"Come on," he said more jovially. "Keep me some braced company. I'm always the only one with these stupid things, especially over the summer, and now travelling with Mom. It's so cool to look at someone and see a flash of that too familiar metal in someone else's mouth. That slight awkwardness they feel." His gaze was soft and deep. "And like I said, I'll tell you all about my braces. If you want."

I swallowed again. Felt the smooth plastic of my retainer arched across the roof of my mouth. I felt so naked and exposed like this. In front of someone I barely knew. And I kind of liked the feeling. It scared me, but I liked it.

4.

I smiled and put my hands down, and gave him an *If you really want me to* shrug.

He beamed.

"I feel pretty stupid," I had to at least complain lispily.

He looked me in the eyes. "Not stupid. Vulnerable, right? And sort of adventurous."

I was caught by his gaze, and then his words. I had to look down, and I blushed. I couldn't even bring out the words that I agreed – I didn't want to agree. But he was exactly right.

"So, OK. Retainers." I bared them, trying not to wince in embarrassment at the way I looked and sounded. "So what's the deal with your braces?" I wanted to exact my pound of flesh in return, at least. Learn why he was in braces for a second round. "Is this really the second time you got them? Why did you ever agree to that? How could you let that happen?"

He laughed unembarrassedly. "I didn't *agree* to get these," he said pointing at his braces. "But it's a long story."

"I have all day," I said. Though feeling my retainers in my mouth I didn't know how long I could – or wanted to – hold out with those.

"So, I got braces when I was in fifth grade," Charles said. "Mom rushed me into them as soon as the dentist said I could get them. To get it over with as soon as possible. So I had them for like a year and a half. By the end of sixth grade I was done. And of course I got retainers – though I got the see-through kind, not the proper ones, with the wire, like you have. I had the kind that are like covers for the teeth. They were really annoying, and they were removable, and, yeah, I didn't wear them like I was supposed to. And pretty soon I didn't wear them at all."

"Your parents didn't notice?"

"You could barely tell whether or not I was wearing them *anyway*. If they had ever asked, I could tell them I was wearing them and they probably would have believed me. But they were much happier not to hear about them, or see them anyway. I don't know about your mom, but mine...well, you see the way she can't help but look disappointed every time she sees my braces, right? So out of sight, out of mind – that was exactly how she preferred to treat my braces and retainers."

"And your orthodontist?"

"Well, the first retainer check, after a couple of months, my teeth hadn't really moved too much. He wasn't happy, and he said I had to wear them regularly, but that went in one ear and out the other. And then we moved, so it wasn't really possible to go back for additional checkups, and my parents thought I was finished with that orthodontic fix anyway, so they didn't really make any effort at any follow through.

"I started seeing a new dentist too, after we moved, and I guess he didn't know my whole history, so he wasn't alarmed right away either. For some reason, it took a while to sink in that everything was moving and getting completely out of shape, and that my teeth needed serious reining in again. A real reset.

"It was only when I got to high school that the dentist said *Whoa!* So I got my braces off at the end of sixth grade, and had basically given up on my retainers by the start of seventh, and I don't think I even knew where they were anymore by eighth grade. So I went through two grades of middle school like a normal kid, and then started high school, and sometime around then my dentist finally told my mother that I should really get my teeth checked by an orthodontist.

"Even then, that took a while to sink in. I think Mom tried to contact my old orthodontist first, but he was like three hours away so it made no sense to go there. Except maybe to blame him for not seeing everything through right. And then it took a couple of more months before Mom organized a new orthodontist, close to where we were now. So it was like spring semester of ninth grade when I had my first orthodontist appointment in close to three years.

"The orthodontist had one of these sleek practices, all white and glass, and a big, long examination room where there were five examination chairs lined up, side by side, each at an angle, looking out into the open through this long glass wall.

"It was kind of neat, to be able to stare into nature at the orthodontist's – but I always wondered what would happen if someone showed up on the other side of the window and started staring in. It must have been inaccessible for some reason, because I never saw anyone out there, but it was still hard to get rid of that feeling there....

"Anyway, we went there, and the orthodontist had Mom and me come into her office, where she looked through my old file from my old orthodontist – my almost three year old file, by then – and she already arched her eyebrows when she asked me for my retainers and I had to admit that I didn't know where they were.

"She didn't say anything, but she stared at me in that intimidating way doctors can when you're not doing what they tell you, and then she called an assistant to take X-rays and all that stuff.

"I remembered most of that from when I first got braces. A weird X-ray, with a cone that swept like across your face, and then the pictures, where you had to hold these clear, plastic tabs that pulled your lips open and apart."

I nodded, remembering exactly what Charles was describing from my own first orthodontic consultation. He was a pretty good storyteller – or maybe I was just happy to be able to keep my mouth closed, hiding my retainers. I certainly *felt* that I was wearing them – but it wasn't that bad. Almost comforting, in a way – if not for the constant nervousness of revealing my wired grin, or saying something and tripping and slurring over all the words.

"Finally, the assistant brought me back into the big, long examination room and had me sit down in one of the chairs, and she prepared that rubbery alginate with which they take impressions of your teeth, right? And so she did that, and then said I should wait.

"I tried not to stare too much at the other patients, but it was kind of cool, because the orthodontist was like some sort of orthodontist to the stars. So I recognized one kid from some TV commercials, and there was a girl in the chair beside me who was on TV like every week. And she was complaining to her mother, who was standing there – or maybe it was her agent? or personal manager? you can never tell in the entertainment business. Anyway, the girl was complaining about the appliance she had to wear, which was one of these removable kinds that you only have to wear at night. But I could see it on the tray in front of her, and it was like both a top and bottom retainer in one, and I could see how that must be pretty uncomfortable.

"When the orthodontist came she went to that girl first, and I could see her putting the appliance in the girl's mouth and checking the fit. She asked the girl a few questions, about whether it hurt here or there, but the girl could like just mumble her response. And then the orthodontist said, 'Well, let's see how this feels. I'll check back in in a couple of minutes.'

"Then she washed her hands and came over to me. She looked at the chart and some of the papers the assistant gave her – like a photograph or maybe already an X-ray, and then she turned on the spotlight, and she did the usual dentist thing of peering around in my mouth. Pulling one side of my lips back, then the other. Having me open and close my mouth. The whole routine."

I nodded. I remembered that when mine did that, I wondered what she was looking for.

"She didn't say anything, and she had a pretty grim look on her face. But I think that was just her professional look. It wasn't like she shouted in horror or even just looked any grimmer when she examined my mouth. But she did not look pleased.

"Then she said I was done and sent me back to the waiting room.

"I couldn't help stare at the girl in the chair next to me when I walked by. She was struggling with the appliance in her mouth, but she looked pretty determined. But you could see from the way she had to hold her mouth, because it was so full, that it must have been really uncomfortable. Like way more than what you're putting up with in your mouth right now.

"Mom looked even more nervous when I joined her in the waiting room, especially when I couldn't report anything. And after a while an assistant called her, to come talk with the orthodontist.

"I was relieved that it was only a really short talk. Obviously they hadn't discussed much. Or decided anything.

"Well?' I asked when Mom came back. Not that I was eager to hear. I mean, there couldn't be any good spin on this, right? Other than the orthodontist telling Mom I was a hopeless case....

"Mom said, 'She still has to go over all the information she collected to make a proper assessment. You have an appointment with her next week, and she'll tell us what she thinks then.'

"So that wasn't great news, but at least it wasn't terrible news. I figured she was going to want me to wear some kind of retainers again, and I just hoped it wasn't like the one I had seen that girl getting.

"I was somewhat nervous that week, but not really much. Mom never brought it up until the night before the appointment, to remind me of it. And I figured I would wait and see. If I really did get a set of new retainers, maybe I'd try to wear them, I told myself. But I didn't even feel I had to.

"Mom was a bit annoyed that the appointment was in the morning on a school day, so I had to miss my first classes, and she had to adjust her schedule, because she was going to have to drop me off at school afterwards. But I didn't think too much of it. I didn't mind missing class. And if I actually did get retainers already at this appointment I could hide them at the bottom of my schoolbag, or even give them to Mom to take home. I didn't even imagine that I would leave the office with anything on my teeth. At worst I thought maybe she'd make me wear the retainers and tell me to keep them in – but I knew I would take them out at the latest when Mom dropped me off. No way was I showing up at school wearing retainers!"

Charles laughed, because we already both knew that things hadn't turned out like he imagined.

"So we get to the practice and sign in and go the waiting room. And it's a bit quieter than last time, because it's school time – and filming time. Lots of the patients are on set someplace, working. Acting. But there are some other patients and parents there. And after a long fifteen minutes or so the assistant calls us to the orthodontist's office.

"We sit down on the other side of her desk. And there's a plaster cast of a set of teeth on the desk and it takes me a moment, but I realize those are *my* teeth. And they really don't look good. Without the lips and cheeks covering them, fully exposed like that, you really see what your teeth look like. And these were not straight, and the arches were like narrow and pointy and it was obvious that they were not the way they were supposed to be.

"So the orthodontist points out the obvious. I hadn't worn my retainers, so my teeth had relapsed. And other things as well. 'And we have to do something about this,' she said after her quick summary.

"She gives me a serious look, and then my mother a serious look. Trying to make clear the orthodontic gravity of the situation. And then she says I should wait in the waiting room while she discusses it with my mother. 'The assistant will come get you when we've decided how to proceed,' she said. 'So please do what she tells you to.'

"On the one hand, I didn't like being left out of this conversation. On the other hand, the last thing I wanted to do was discuss what orthodontic options were open to us, and to be reminded how I couldn't be trusted about wearing my retainers. I was sure Mom was going to remind her that that had been so long ago, and that I had matured, and I'd probably be much better about wearing them now. But let's face it, I didn't want retainers or anything else.

"I don't know what simple solution and escape from all this I was hoping for or maybe even expecting, but somehow I still expected that it couldn't be that bad.

"After like ten minutes my Mom still hasn't come out of the office, but an assistant comes and smiles and says I should follow her. So I do, and she leads me into the long examination room and we walk by the other chairs and patients – there are like two of them, and I catch the eye of one who is staring miserably at the two pink Hawley retainers on the tray in front of him, waiting for him. But I tell myself that if I get something like those – well, I'll manage somehow.

"The assistant leads me all the way to the end of the room, to the last chair and has me lie down there, and she adjusts it so I am half sitting up, and she clips one of those paper napkins around my neck, and then she walks away again.

"So I have the usual butterflies you have when you're in the chair at the dentist's, waiting for the dentist. But I tell myself, it can't be too bad.

"And then I see the assistant come back, and there's something dangling from her hand. Beige strips, not very long, but with some metal, and some white fluff on parts of them. And I had no idea what it was, but she wasn't stopping at any of the other chairs, she was coming back to mine. It was too big to wear – even for some strange headgear – so it wasn't anything orthodontic. But I couldn't identify it, or figure out what it was for.

"And she put one down, whatever this was, on the tray beside me and she took the other one and put it near the end of my left armrest.

"Now I could see it was some sort of leather strap. Maybe two inches wide, and there was a two inch square of it which was connected to two maybe six inch strips of leather on opposing sides of it, all of which now dangled over the armrest. I watched her thread the bottom strip on each side through a small metal clip on each side of the bottom of the armrest, and then buckle it closed, like a belt buckle. I realized that secured the straps to the armrest.

"The top two strips, which were still dangling freely were a bit different. They had a white, fluffy layer on one side, and a slightly different type of belt-buckle at the ends.

"And then I realized what this was. Just as the assistant gently took my wrist and guided it to the leather bit. She wanted to strap my hand down.

"I practically jumped up – well, I just sat up a bit, in shock. 'Wait,' I said. 'Is this really necessary?'

"The assistant looked at me with a smile, like she couldn't believe I was kicking up a fuss about such an insignificant thing. 'Doctor's orders,' she said. And when my shocked expression didn't change, she added, 'You're the boy who didn't wear his retainers like he was supposed to, right? Yeah, I don't think you want to aggravate the doctor any more than you already have. Besides, it's not uncomfortable. You'll see.'

"But if I *saw* it would be too late. But still, lying there, in a doctor's office, with someone in a lab coat working on you, it's kind of intimidating and you go along with what they say and so I gave up any resistance and let her guide my hand onto the armrest. With my hand I could hold onto the end of the armrest, while she pulled the two straps around my wrist and threaded the end of one in the buckle of the other and then pulled until the soft lining was closed tight around my wrist and then she buckled it closed.

"I wiggled my arm back and forth, but my wrist was firmly held in place. There was a bit of give, but not much. My hand was strapped down.

"And then she did the other side, and I let her, and I couldn't believe this was happening. I was helpless. Stuck.

"Looking around at the other chairs I noticed the other patients' hands weren't strapped down. They hadn't been the first time I was here either – I would have noticed. I even feebly protested to the assistant, but she just smiled and said, 'Well, patients who don't wear their retainers get a bit more attention. The doctor wants to make sure they get the message.'

"I wasn't sure about the message. Or what to expect next. But I knew I was more or less immobilized. And while it wasn't like I would have ever dared jump out of the examination chair anyway, it felt different knowing that, no matter what, I couldn't."

I nodded, transfixed by Charles's story – and knowing exactly how he had felt. Charles gave me a questioning look, and a moment to interrupt him, but I shook my head and let him continue. I couldn't wait to hear the rest of this.

"So it was a bit embarrassing to be restrained like this – though I was surprised to realize it wasn't really that uncomfortable. It kind of did away with the usual problem at the dentist, of what to do with your hands, which was actually sort of better.

"I imagined that maybe the orthodontist thought I was so unreliable that she wanted to make sure I couldn't take out whatever retainers she had planned for me right then and there. Or that she wanted to remind me very forcefully of who was boss, in order to convince me to be more conscientious about wearing my retainers this time around.

"I was a bit annoyed that nobody was telling me what was going on, and that I had to wait. But waiting was still better than anything happening. Looking at the next patient over, two seats from mine, with another orthodontist or an assistant working on his wide open mouth it definitely seem preferable to get to wait. And I was relieved that no one seemed to notice that I had been strapped down.

"The assistant came back and sat down on the dentist's stool and explained that she was going to clean my teeth a bit. 'Just to make sure they're presentable,' she said.

"I wasn't worried by this. An assistant going over your teeth and picking and cleaning was something that seemed to happen at every dentist's visit. This wasn't that different – except when she had me rinse and spit it was slightly more complicated, because my hands were tied down. So she had to pour the water in my mouth, and then pull that rinse-bowl right up under my chin for me to spit out. But she did it deftly, so she must have been used to working with patients in a position similar to mine.

"When she went to get a cheek retractor I was sort of surprised. You know, one of those lip spreaders, with the grooves in the side which your lips go in, and then it spreads your mouth all wide open? But I couldn't really protest or anything, and before I knew it she had it in my mouth and my lips were spread totally open. Then she hooked the vacuum tube over the side, and turned it on, to suck the saliva out of my mouth.

"Since she went on scraping and poking at my teeth, I assumed it was just because this way they were more exposed and it was easier for her to work with them. I had no idea what she was spreading and buffing, and why she had to get to all of my teeth, but she did a really thorough job.

"Finally she seemed to be finished, and she turned off the spotlight shining on my mouth. 'OK,' she said. 'All done for now. The orthodontist will be with you soon.'

"And then she left me like that. My mouth held wide open. So I couldn't move my hands, and now I couldn't really speak. It wasn't awfully uncomfortable. But obviously I felt really exposed, and annoyed that I had to wait like this. And kind of nervous.

"It's like another five minutes before the orthodontist comes, with my mother walking reluctantly behind her. I'm kind of embarrassed for my mom to see me like this, but on the other hand I'm glad she's there to get this situation to a resolution, so we can get out of here.

"The orthodontist sits down on the stool beside me and turns the spotlight on again, and she peers at my mouth and then smiles at me. 'Not too uncomfortable, I hope?' she says. Of course I can only gurgle in response.

"I look at Mom, who almost looks afraid to step too close. She's trying to smile encouragingly, but she looks like she's feeling really guilty too. Like she should be, I think to myself, putting me in this position.

"'So as I understand it, you had trouble wearing your retainers like you were supposed to,' the orthodontist said to me. But she was like all friendly, not even accusing me. 'So we're going to have to fix some things, since we've had quite a bit of movement, without those retainers to hold everything in their proper place. And this time, we'll make it easier for you. So there's not as much responsibility on your shoulders. OK?'

"I didn't know – and didn't want to guess what she meant. And I couldn't really respond anyway. She looked at me for a moment, and my blank look was apparently answer enough for her anyway. She turned to my mother and pointed at my mouth. 'You can see pretty clearly how much intervention is necessary, right? That there really aren't any alternatives.'

"Mom nodded grimly, and the orthodontist cheerfully said, 'Well, then let's get started.'

"An assistant wheeled over a cabinet with all sorts of narrow drawers and utensils and things on top of it. The orthodontist adjusted the chair so that I was lying almost flat now, and then she smiled at Mom and said, 'You might as well wait in the waiting room. It shouldn't take too long.'

"Not too long…that at least sounded good to me. Maybe she was fitting me with some kind of complicated retainer? Well, if it was over fast it couldn't be too bad.

"Mom gave me a sad look and put her hand on my forearm. 'I'm sorry, Charles, but we talked it over and this really seems the only option.' But she wouldn't spell out what that option was….

"So she walked away and the orthodontist turned her attention to me, and all I could do was lie there and let her do whatever she was going to do. And I still had no idea what that was.

"She began by preparing the back molars, There was another sort of liquid to brush over them, and then she got out a metal band, and she tried it in for size, and then prepared some other substance which she like smeared inside it, and then she forced it over my molar. And I kind of understood that what she was doing was cementing a molar band on. And I was kind of disappointed, because obviously this meant I wasn't just getting a simple retainer, but probably something more complicated, with the molar bands there to anchor it somehow or something. I couldn't tell how it might work, but that was my reasoning.

"She continued with all by back molars, top and bottom, so first there were four banded molars, and then I was a bit surprised when she did the next ones over, too, and so there were eight. But these were all teeth at the back of my mouth, so I still figured they were just there to help hold the retainers in place, and this was going to be annoying, because I had these permanent metal bits in the back of my mouth. But it didn't seem like it would be the end of the world.

"This procedure was different from when I had gotten braces the first time, because I didn't have any bands at all with those. It was all brackets, cemented to the front of my teeth. But even if this procedure was kind of annoying, it wasn't terrible. And when she had done the eight bands she pulled back and took her latex gloves off and looked at me like she was finished. I mean, I assumed there were still retainers to come, and a lecture to go with them, but that that would be that.

"She got up to check on some other patients – I guess she wanted to let the cement set and so on too, and so I sat there with my mouth open and my hands tied down. It could have been worse, I told myself – and I started to get curious about the retainers I was getting, and how she better not say that I should wear them during the daytime too, even if it was only for a breaking-in period.

"So after ten or fifteen minutes she comes back, and I look around to see if she's carrying anything, or her assistant is bringing anything, and I'm kind of relieved they aren't – and I wonder if maybe she'll only finish up at another appointment.

"But she sits down again, and turns on the spotlight on my mouth, bathing it in warm light. And she begins brushing a pungent substance on one of my teeth, and then picks up a bracket out of a small tray and brushes something on the back of that, and presses it against my teeth.

"Now this process I recognize. It's not exactly how my old orthodontist did it, but this was what had happened when I first got braces. And I just looked at her in disbelief.

This can't be happening, I told myself. Is she putting braces on my teeth?

"And when it was only one I could sort of believe maybe something else was going on, but when she starts doing one tooth after another I realize there is just no way around it. I was getting braces. Braces were being put on my teeth. A full set of metal braces. I couldn't see the brackets and the bands she was installing very clearly before they disappeared in my mouth, but the all-metal silver glitter as she brought them to my mouth was crystal clear.

"I was in total shock. It had never occurred to me I could be getting braces. I realized how stupid I was in thinking that – of course braces were one of the obvious solutions! I just hadn't seen the extent of the problem.

"So I'm lying there, and there's nothing I can do. I can wriggle my hands, but they are held down without any give. And in a way I'm glad they are, because even if they were free, what was I going to do? I would never have the nerve to push her away and get up and run away. No, the braces were going to happen, and at least I was completely helpless about it and I could convince myself that there was nothing I could do.

"But my head was spinning. *This can't be happening to me*, I kept thinking over and over, as she cheerily affixed one bracket after another to my teeth. *As it was happening*, in other words. I couldn't even imagine that I was going to get up out of this seat, and I was going to have braces.

"I couldn't even really think ahead. Or I think I blocked it out. The thought of showing up at school in braces – it was too much for my mind to handle. Hell, this was too much for my mind to handle.

"And the orthodontist kept working away, like my mouth was some assembly line and she was working her way across one row and then another.

"After she had done a lot of them she called over one of the nearby assistants and said that she should send over one of the patients being worked on when they were done with her. I could feel the orthodontist press the brackets to one of my front incisors when the assistant led a girl who was a couple of years younger than me over.

"The orthodontist greeted her, and said something like, 'You've been having some trouble with your retainers, right? Not wearing them all the time you should, right?'

"The girl sort of shrugged and nodded at the same time. When she said 'I guess,' I could see – and hear – the retainers she was wearing. They were like yours, with the wire....

"The orthodontist stopped what she was doing for a moment and turned to the girl and said, 'Well take a good look. This young man had braces when he was your age, and then he got retainers like you, but he didn't wear them like he was supposed to, and now he's back getting braces. Except now he's in high school...'

"The girl literally shuddered as she looked at me, truly scared that such a fate was possible. I had no idea how I looked, but if the look in her eyes was any indication, it wasn't anything good.

"The orthodontist continued to give her a talking-to, half encouragement, half warning. The girl looked impressed – and intimidated.

"When the orthodontist had sent her off she winked at me and said, 'Maybe we helped scare her straight,' she said. 'So some additional good comes out of this.'

"Finally she was all done with the brackets, and she left me there to stew for a few more minutes, maybe for the glue to really set, or just to stretch her legs some.

"On the one hand my mind was racing, while on the other I felt paralyzed. And I *was* immobilized – which was probably for the best. I couldn't and I didn't want to move. At least lying there I was in weird orthodontia-world. Once I had to get up and step into the real world the nightmare would really hit home.

"The orthodontist came back and got the archwires, and she stretched them across the brackets and forced them into the grooves in them. She had to wire the archwires in with a really thin wire and some pliers on the molar bands, but the brackets on my teeth are kind of cool. They have like a little metal shutter that closes over the slot in which the archwire lies."

Charles leaned forward with his mouth open to show me. Peering more closely at them I could see what he meant. They did look kind of cool. Though more metallic, too, than when there were the rubber band ligatures on each tooth. But it was also because the brackets were pretty large for braces. They covered more surface area on his teeth than my braces had, for example.

"So she shuts all these little doors over the archwire with this special tool she has for it," Charles continued, "which goes pretty fast, and I can almost immediately feel that slight tension from the braces starting to work. I could feel it. I definitely had braces.

"Then she gets two of those small round elastics out of a small baggie, and she stretches one between the top and bottom rows of braces one each side of my mouth. Like I still have now. I never had those with my first set of braces, but I could feel the added tension they caused.

"'I think we're all done,' the orthodontist said cheerfully and proudly. And I'm like someone who has just been clubbed on the head with an anvil. I can't believe what has happened.

"The orthodontist didn't remove the cheek retractor yet, so I couldn't really tell how the braces felt, but she raised the chair so that I was now almost sitting upright again. She got a pretty large mirror, which she propped on the tray hovering in front of me, and then she adjusted that so that I could see myself.

"And so there I get my first look at…this. Not just this, but, you know, with the cheek retractor my lips are pulled totally apart so everything is exposed and I see the full horror. Even now, if I like bare my teeth, you only see most of the braces, but here I was faced with my reflection like a foot in front of me, and all I saw was this black hole of braces where my mouth had been.

"I was just dumbfounded. They were bigger and more imposing than my first set of braces had been. And they were braces! I looked so totally different with them.

"You probably remember when you first got a look at your braces, right? Did you burst out in tears?"

I remembered it well. The orthodontist had given me a handheld mirror and I really had burst into tears as soon as I saw what I looked like. I couldn't stop sobbing. Even though I was sort of prepared for what was coming. But you can never imagine what they'll look like on your own face. And Charles's were even more imposing than mine had been.

"And you at least had some time to mentally prepare for what was coming," Charles reminded me. "I had no idea. And suddenly I had them – and I saw what I looked like with them. I was too shocked to even cry.

"I looked helplessly at the orthodontist, but of course by then it was too late. Too late for anything. And she was just smiling at me like this was the greatest thing in the world. Like she had corrected some incredible wrong.

"And then she said, 'Let's leave the cheek retractor in, so we can show your mom,' and she went to get Mom, leaving me like that, my mouth all exposed and the mirror right in front of me, so I couldn't look away, all I could see was my horribly new braced face staring back at me."

I couldn't stop staring at Charles's braces while he talked. I rarely had a chance to see braces up close like this for so long. Even my friends who had them tended to hide them when they talked, behind their hands of hair, or trying not to open their mouths so much. Or they didn't talk as much at all anyway. And naturally we tried not to stare. But here it seemed OK too, and it was weird because Charles's braces were both awful and neat. Like how he had showed me how the brackets were different than the usual ones with the ligatures. And listening to his story, I could just imagine what it must have been like for him to get these, and then to see himself – like this! – for the first time.

"And then my mom came over," Charles said, "and I could see the panic in her eyes when she first saw me. She tried to smile, but you could see how horrified she was. Of course.

"And the orthodontist showed her my braces. Telling her I needed to wear these elastics all the time. And she pointed to the bands on my back molars, and pointed out there were tubes there. 'That's where the headgear will go,' she said. So now I knew I was getting headgear too. I hadn't had headgear the first time I had braces, but now I was getting headgear too....

"Mom looked as stunned as I felt, and she didn't say anything, and the orthodontist smiled at me and said she was going to talk over some things with Mom, and she'd be back soon.

"And she left me there, with my mouth still wide pen. I couldn't say anything. I could just look at my reflection. She must have done it on purpose, so I'd get used to what I looked like, but it was still such a shock to the system....

"Then this girl came over, who was like a year or two younger than me, and she had a really big retainer case in one hand, in which you could hear some devices rattling, but she didn't have anything in her mouth. And she was curious, so she came over to me, and when she looked at my mouth her eyes grew all wide.

"She said something like, 'Wow!' and she asked me whether I had just had them installed. I nodded and she like laughed and said, 'You really got the works didn't you? And you're like in high school, aren't you? Wow, that must be rough. High school with those....'

"And I hadn't even thought about that, but of course she was right. I knew my life was over. Life at school was over. I had braces – braces that looked like this. I was at the bottom rung, knocked off any ladder I might have made my way up over the years. A special kind of loser.

"Then the girl noticed my hands were tied down, and her eyes grew even wider. 'Man, they had to tie your hands down?' she said.

"The orthodontist came back, and the girl asked her whether all the patients that got braces installed had their hands restrained.

"'It depends on the patient and the length of the procedure,' the orthodontist explained. 'It helps keep the patients from fidgeting,' she said. 'I'm sure Charles didn't mind,' she said, smiling at me.

"'My sister is getting braces like that, right?' the girl said. 'Are you going to strap her hands down for that?'

"'Do you think we should?' the orthodontist asked, and the girl smiled an evil smile and said, 'Definitely!'

"Even the orthodontist smiled at that. And the girl continued to stare at me – at my braces. And then she noticed the tubes on the molar bands, and she asked, 'Oh my God! is he getting headgear too?'

"The orthodontist nodded, and the girl just shook her head pityingly, and I felt like the whole world was going to look at me like this from now on. Which was so not a good feeling.

"Finally the orthodontist sat back down, and unhooked the vacuum tube, and took out the cheek retractor, and my lips slowly closed – except at first I could hardly feel them, because they had been stretched to capacity for so long. But then I felt the braces – against the insides of my cheeks, and with my tongue, and instead of the smooth surfaces of my teeth I had all this barbed wire now, and I was still just in total shock.

"'So do you have any questions, Charles?' the orthodontist said all cheerfully, but my only question was how could this happen to me, and I couldn't really ask that. The orthodontist babbled on about how I probably knew how to take care of my braces from the first time I had them, and what I could eat or drink or do with them, and how I had to wear the elastics, and that she had given my mom all the instruction sheets about them. And then she finally unstrapped my hands and let me get up, and she said she was looking forward to seeing me in a couple of weeks and let me go.

"I staggered out of the examination room, not even noticing the other patients in the other chairs, and lurched over to my mom, who was waiting in the waiting room, and I was still totally speechless.

"'I'm so sorry, Charles,' she said, shaking her head – not as an apology for what she had let them do to me, but because she felt so sorry for what I had been turned into. And I still couldn't say anything. I was so overwhelmed by what had happened to me.

"I saw the girl with the retainer case sitting in the waiting room next to her mom, and when she saw me she actually pointed and leaned over and said something to her mom, and I could just imagine how she and the whole wide world were now going to be talking about me and what I looked like. Everywhere I went.

"When we buckled our seatbelts in the car, before we drove off, Mom turned to me again and said, 'Let me see,' again, and I reluctantly bared her teeth, and you could see her flinch when she saw the metal mess that now covered my teeth.

"'I didn't think they'd be so bad,'" she admitted, speaking as much to herself as to me.

"Finally, once we started driving, I spluttered, 'How could you do this to me?'

"And she was all, "Really, there was no choice. I talked it over with the orthodontist and she explained that we really had no other option. And there was no good reason to wait any longer, so we decided we might as well bite the bullet and get them on right away.'

"And I shook my head. 'Couldn't we have talked about it?' I asked.

"But she insisted, 'There was nothing to talk about. You need braces. She said the previous orthodontist, he just did the essential things, and if you had worn your retainers that might have been good enough, but the combination of the original treatment not tackling everything he should have, and your not wearing your retainers – well, it means there's a lot that needs correcting. Like it would have been better if you had had headgear originally – I remember your orthodontist mentioned that, but I didn't want to inflict that on you unless it was absolutely necessary, so he didn't use it. But now you're definitely going to need it.'

"'I can't get headgear!' I said, but Mom just said, 'You already have those braces, so it really isn't that much more. And you really do need it, she says, and if you don't wear it

– well, the alternative appliances she can use are even worse, and will keep you in braces even longer.'

"Which reminded me to ask, 'And how long am I supposed to have these?'

"She's not sure yet. It depends on a lot of things, including your cooperation. But maybe not much more than year or a year and a half.' But any amount of time she said – even the promise of getting them off the next day would have seemed too long for me.

"Only then did it sink in that we were driving to school. It was barely noon, and Mom was sending me back to school. With braces. I protested, but she said I shouldn't be ridiculous. I was going to have to get used to having them, and people seeing me with them. What choice did I have?

"She didn't realize that showing up in braces at school meant, more or less, the end of my life. Of my life as a normal, average teenager anyway. I was going to be a laughingstock. A loser. A kids with *braces*.

"At least I was in a different school from when I had first had braces, with different friends. No one knew or remembered that I had already had them. That would have been too humiliating. Not that this wasn't, by itself....

"So Mom dropped me off at school, and I slowly made my way back in. Stopping to take deep breaths. Gritting my teeth – which were already hurting – to make sure I didn't cry. Though I'm sure my eyes were all glistening and red.

"Of course it was as bad and worse than I anticipated. Everyone noticed. Everyone laughed and joked. Everyone said something. And even if people didn't mean anything bad, I was in such a heightened state of self-pity that I interpreted every glance as someone looking down on me because of my braces.

"You remember what it was like, right? I mean, you can't help it. You think you're the biggest joke going, right, regardless of how anyone reacts."

I nodded. Braces heightened your self-consciousness to an unbelievable degree. At least they did mine – and apparently Charles's too.

"You must have been so furious at your mom," I said.

Charles nodded. "But it was more like I was furious at the whole world, for picking on me like this. Mom was just doing her small part. It was like a conspiracy to ridicule me. To make me the most pathetic person possible. And of course I felt it was partially my fault too, because I hadn't worn my retainers – but I also felt it was unfair that I had been expected to do the impossible. The braces felt like they weren't just a punishment for my failure, but a punishment for just being *me*."

I was surprised how much Charles's words resonated. My parents treated my getting braces like it was just the natural order of things, but to me it also felt like a failure on my part – my teeth just a visible sign of all my imperfection – and a punishment. A pretty awful punishment.

"You seem pretty comfortable with your braces now, though," I said. "Pretty confident. You're not hiding them or anything."

Charles looked surprised. "Are you kidding? You had braces. Did you ever feel comfortable with them? In public? Did you ever reach a point where you weren't self-conscious around others?"

I shook my head. Of course not. That had been a long, embarrassing two years. "But you seem OK having them."

He arched his eyebrows even more, like he was taken aback. "No. I've made my peace with having them. I've made the best of it. I even like having them, at times. But I'll never be comfortable with having them. I don't think anyone ever could be."

"You like having them?" I said, genuinely surprised.

"Sure. The feel of them in my mouth. The gentle ache, when they don't hurt too much. When I'm lying in bed at night. Even the tug of the headgear."

I could understand and even relate to what he said. I never wanted to admit it to myself when I had braces, those moments and sensations of pleasure. Besides, the misery of having them always seemed to drown these out. But there was something to what he said. If you closed your eyes and closed out the world, that mouthful of braces or even the retainers could, briefly, be bliss. Not that I could ever admit that to anyone. I could barely admit it to myself.

"It's just around other people that the self-consciousness overwhelms everything else," he said. "It's hard to carve out places and situations where you can enjoy the braces for themselves. Everyone else is so judgmental."

"You didn't have any trouble putting on the headgear yesterday," I reminded him.

"Are you kidding?" he said. "Do you know how hard it was for me to screw up my courage to put that on and wear it in front of you?"

"Really?"

"Are you kidding? I could never wear it in front of my friends or anyone I knew. And even here – especially here – I was mortified."

"So why...?"

"I told you. For one, to get the moms off our backs. It wiped any worries they might have had about us getting up to any mischief if we were left alone, right? So I get to spend the day with you, instead of driving around with them. But really I did it more to take advantage of the situation. I'm far from home. I have the chance to expose myself completely to another person, without worrying about what she thinks a week or a month from now. I mean, you'll always remember me like this, right?" He bared his ultra-braced teeth. "All braces. And the headgear. But that's who I am right now, at this point in my life. It's kind of cool to openly be able to share that with someone – something I would never dare do at home."

"Why me?" I said. Annoyed by the slight trembling in my voice. I hoped the retainer-slurred speech covered that up.

"You had braces, so you understand what I'm going through. You're willing to wear your retainers...."

He reached forward and brushed my lips ever so gently with the tip of his index finger. I tried not to move, or to react. It was the most intimate gesture I had ever experienced. I had made out with boys before. Fumbling, awkward, and usually beer-breathed lip-locking, and nothing had ever felt like that simple, light touch had.

But he was a boy with *braces*, I reminded myself....

"I would never be able to open up, to share, not like this, if you didn't have those in your mouth," Charles said.

I blushed. My retainers had never been good for anything – except that keeping my teeth straight stuff... – but he sounded like he really meant it. "Why not?" I asked. Glad that it was only the two words, so the quivering of my voice wasn't too obvious.

"Initially, partly, because if you didn't I'd feel so unequal, me in braces and you not. It's too different a world. Like the way almost everyone else sees me. Even if you had experienced it, had had braces – without anything left in your mouth, the humiliating traces revealing themselves every time you open your mouth, you'd just suppress any memory of what it was like.

"But", he continued, "it's also what they do to you even beyond that. That vulnerability you can't hide when you're wearing them is part of it. And then there's your beauty."

Now I was really blushing.

"You're a really pretty girl," Charles said earnestly, staring into my eyes so deeply that I couldn't look away. "But without the retainers, you're like any pretty girl. The retainers – the silver wires across your teeth, the way they affect your speech – are small imperfections that make all that inner and outer beauty shine even more brightly. Blindingly brightly."

My face deep red, I still managed to protest – though I couldn't get the smile off my face. "I don't think *anyone* has ever seen that.". Which was certainly true. Certainly no one had ever said or suggested anything like that.

Charles laughed. "But you never really let them see it, do you? The only people who have seen you with those things are everyone who saw you after you had your braces. When you got the braces off and then had to show up wearing those. And were deeply ashamed of them, every moment that you had them. But me, I got to see you without them first. I got to see the normal girl you try to present yourself as to the world. And now you've let me peek behind that façade and revealed the vulnerable, real part of yourself that you now keep hidden from everyone else. So I can see your full, incredible beauty – which is enhanced by the wires holding you back, the plastic stunting your speech.

"I am someone who can understand it, who can see…not beyond the retainers, but at least not *just* the retainers, like everyone else would. Because I have to face the world every day wearing these things," he said, pointing at his braces, "and I know that while they're the visible, essential part of me, the part that makes the first and most lasting impression, they're only part of the surface. And though their hold goes really deep, I know there's a lot more to me there as well."

He paused for a moment. "And I see…I dare hope, that maybe someone who is willing to reveal herself with her own embarrassing retainers – which she doesn't have to show anyone – can see that too."

I felt a bit hot and faint. I wasn't sure what I was feeling. There really was a connection there. I really believed him when he spoke of my beauty – even when he said he saw it in what everyone else had always considered such an ugly metal manifestation.

It reminded me of things I had tried to forget, or tried to convince myself I didn't believe. Like those times I had looked in the mirror, happy about the look of those straight wires running neatly across my teeth. Or when I had gone to bed, glad to have the comforting and reassuring feel of the plastic inside my mouth.

What made the retainers so hard, so impossible to bear, was not so much them themselves, but being seen and heard in them, and the laughter and pity of everyone who saw me with them. But Charles seemed to be able to see them differently….

My heart pounded in my chest, and my mind raced. This was so confusing. It was unlike any experience I had ever had. Unlike any conversation with even the most sympathetic friend, or my parents. And it was so strange to be wearing my retainers at the same time – something I always hoped so desperately to leave behind me, or at least tuck into a hidden corner of my life that I could keep secret from anyone – especially anyone I liked. And here was Charles, who liked nothing better than to have them fully out into the open, in my mouth. And Charles...but I looked at him, and his braces – because he *was* his braces – and I couldn't imagine being drawn to him. Because...braces. There. In the way. A joke.

And yet beyond and aside from the braces I could feel myself very strongly drawn to him. And, if I was being honest with myself – even the braces....

"So you said you made the best of having braces," I said, my voice breaking as I spoke. But I forced myself to continue. "How did you do that?"

5.

"After I got the braces," Charles said, "I became...well, like any kid who gets braces. You try to pretend it's no big deal, and that you don't notice how everyone stares and smirks and makes fun of you behind your back. Or to your braced face. But deep down you feel as small as can be, the lowest of the low. Your parents tell you they're just braces, and they're not so bad, and it's not for so long, but every braced minute is...well, a braced minute, which is a braced eternity.

"People try to tell you otherwise. *Having braces is no big deal.* Or they try to convince you they don't mind having them. But it's all empty bluster.

"Wasn't it that way for you?" Charles asked. "You have friends who don't seem to mind having braces, but then when you get them – you minded every moment you had them, right?"

I nodded. Exactly.

"And at some point you probably realized your friends minded just as much. They just pretended better. But you pretended too, right?"

I nodded. Of course. I would have rather died than let on how humiliating it was having braces. And he was probably right. We probably all played that same game, trying to fool ourselves and each other.

"So I conformed to expectations," Charles said. "I was less sure of myself. I felt worth less. I certainly felt I didn't belong with the cool kids – and that definition, of the group I felt I didn't belong to, kept expanding. It wasn't like anyone came out and said I was a freak or something. But of course that was how I felt. And we all sort of pretended everything was normal – but when it really came down to it, we all knew that those of us with braces are different, and didn't really belong."

I caught myself nodding, recognizing those exact feelings from my own braced days. I never felt I fit in – or could fit in – as long as I looked like *that*. Even alongside friends in braces! It was impossible to share that humiliation. We each bore it on our own.

"What made it even harder," Charles said, "was that if I managed to get over wallowing in my misery, when I was alone in my room, or lying in bed, trying to fall asleep or trying not to wake up, I realized I *liked* my braces."

He looked at me as if he was afraid his admission would be too great a shock for me. But I couldn't even really react, listening to him with bated breath – and stunned to hear that someone had those same secret feelings I had had, and had tried to suppress.

"Of course they were annoying when I ate, and my teeth ached, and the elastics pulling my jaw together were a pain. But those were also good, enjoyable feelings. Even the pain – like picking at a scab.

"And it was frustrating, because that positive feeling – it withered right away in public. Just seeing someone's expression when they caught sight of my braces – it overwhelmed any good feelings I could have. And the positives people tried to see in them – *It's great you're getting your teeth fixed!* – were all of that sort of clinical, distant sort, pointing out I was going through something nasty but saying it was OK because at least when it was over something positive had come of it."

"But you seem pretty at ease about them now," I had to tell him. "Confident. The way you act and talk – and don't try to hide your braces."

Charles smiled. "Part of it is an act. A lot of it is you – wanting to open up to someone, and wanting that someone to be you, and being so relieved that you have those retainers in your mouth."

I almost didn't blush, but I couldn't help but smile.

"But I also came to two really big realizations, and they turned everything around."

Now I was really curious and I sat up even more.

"The first one was that I admitted to myself that I liked having braces. Or parts about having braces. Going to school with them was still a daily walk of shame, and I knew it always would be – but lots of things about being in school are unpleasant and we're powerless to change them. So I told myself I wouldn't let that, or the way my parents looked at me all pityingly, or anything else take away from what I could get out of them. By myself, usually. At home. Cut off from the world, and in my own little braced world, but at least it was an island of peace and surprising happiness I could withdraw to.

"But I figured it out, and began acting accordingly, somewhere else. I had had my braces for like a month, and it had been one long miserable experience. Or a seemingly endless series of miserable experiences, of people seeing me in braces and saying or not saying things, of how they treated me or how I perceived them treating me, and how I now acted – like I wasn't worthy of being treated normally any longer.

"I was really down and unhappy. No hope, no light in sight. Just these horrific rows of metal staring back at me when I looked in the mirror.

"And then came my next appointment at the orthodontist. It had been more than four weeks, so my teeth didn't hurt at all anymore – and now my mom was dragging me back to the orthodontist, who was obviously going to change the archwires and set me back to a couple of days of aching, frustrating pain. Where you can't chew on anything. Like had happened every five or six weeks when I had had braces the first time. Adding injury – even if it was pretty temporary – to the constant insult that were my braces.

"So we go to the orthodontist, and eventually the assistant calls my name to come get me, and fortunately Mom stays sitting – she still feels guilty about what happened the last time, and can't bear to watch whatever the orthodontist has planned this time.

"The assistant walks me past the first two patients and shows me to an examination chair, and I sit down, and she puts the napkin around my neck and adjusts the chair a bit. And she says, 'The orthodontist will see you soon.'

"And I shrug unhappily, resigning myself to the inevitable. The routine I was going to have to get used to. Me passive, being worked on and then sent back out into the world, newly rewired.

"But as I'm lying there, something clicks in my mind and I actually have the nerve to call out to the assistant, who has already started to walk away. And I sit up a bit and I ask her, 'No straps for the hands today?'

"She comes back over and smiles. 'No,' she explains. 'The orthodontist usually only brings those out for the installment procedure. With patients who might need a bit of extra reinforcement, when they're getting their braces. So don't worry,' she says, like she's pleased to lift a load off my mind.

"But I work up all my nerve and I say, 'Maybe it's better if you do use them again.' I can't bring myself to right out and *ask* that she strap my hands down, but I hope she gets the hint.

"She looks at me for a moment. Trying to look like she doesn't think I'm crazy. And then she very slowly asks, 'Are you sure?' Because she wants to be really sure.

"And I nod my head, like it's not something I like, but I know it's good for me so I'll put up with it, and I tell her, 'Yeah, I think so.'

"Probably if she had said anything else, like an incredulous *Really?* I would have backed down and said I was just joking but she nodded and walked away. And came back with the same straps as last time, and attached them to the armrest. And I put my wrists down in place, and let her tighten the loop around them, and then they were secured in place again."

I listened to Charles with my mouth open, so caught up in his stories that I almost forgot about my retainers. I couldn't believe what he was telling me – even as I understood where he was coming from.

"The first moment, when I could feel how I couldn't pull my arms up, I wondered to myself, *What am I thinking?* But then lying there, I did feel better. Calmer.

"In fact, I realized I felt better than I had since any time I got my braces. Even when I sort of enjoyed having the braces, by myself at home, that feeling had always been accompanied by a sense of guilt and shame, and was almost overwhelmed by the memory of what everyone else thought. But here, in this orthodontic environment, for once my braces didn't matter. They sort of belonged. It was already different in the waiting room, but here, lying next to a few other braced patients, it was OK to have these stupid things, and to look like this.

"That was nice. To lie there, and be *happy*, for the first time in so long.

"It was a while before the orthodontist came over, and I saw the assistant whisper something as they both looked over before she came up to me. About the restraints, I guessed.

"The orthodontist smiled and sat down on the stool beside me and consulted her chart and turned on the spotlight shining on my mouth.

"'So how are you adjusting to the braces?' she asked in a friendly way.

"I shrugged. There was no point in complaining about all the things that were irritating about them, was there? She knew exactly what it was like to have braces, and what annoyed kids about them.

"She asked me whether anything hurt or any wires poked me particularly unpleasantly, and then she did the usual mouth inspection, pulling my lips back, having me bit down. 'Looks like we're off to a good start,' she said. 'Getting things back on track.'

"Finally, when she sits up again, looking down on me, still all friendly, she asks, 'So you think the restraints are a good idea?'

"I gulped and nodded. Pretending I was a bit reluctant and ambivalent about it, but that like some bitter medicine I knew it was good for me.

"She nodded and it didn't look like she was judging me. 'Should I put down that we should always use them?' she asked.

"'Yeah, I guess,' I told her. Trying not to sound too relieved.

"'OK then,' she said, and she wrote something down on her clipboard. And so every time since then the assistant always has the straps ready or even set up on the armrests already and it's like part of the procedure – lie down, napkin around the neck, wrists strapped in."

Listening to Charles, I might have actually whispered *Wow*. I understood his sense of relief, and why he welcomed that added bit of security at every appointment. I even envied him a bit for it.

"Then she asked me whether I had minded that she had used me to set an example," Charles continued. "Bringing patients over to see what was in store for them if they didn't wear their retainers.

"And I tried to look as unbothered as possible, like it was nothing. It had been something – but I realized that here, in this protected environment, it was OK. So I even encouraged her. 'I don't mind,' I told her. 'So if you want to put me on display or teach some of your patients a lesson, go ahead. I'm in no rush anyway – it doesn't bother me to lie here a little longer – and if it helps keep other kids on the straight and narrow, go for it.'

"She looked pleased, though maybe not totally convinced. But then she put the cheek retractor in and started changing the archwires, and along the way she did have another patient come over to take a look at all the stuff installed in my mouth, and when she was done she asked me again and I told her it was totally OK, and she could do that anytime.

"So she does now. I think she even schedules some kids' appointments when she knows I'll be there. And with my hands strapped down, that makes a big impression on the kids too. So I seem to be a useful learning tool for her patients. A useful bad example."

"You really don't mind the staring and stuff?" I asked.

Charles shrugged. "It's different when you're lying in the examination chair. Even with that cheek retractor holding your mouth open. You're like a medical display unit. It's not nearly as uncomfortable as just the way a stranger looks at me on the street when they see my braces."

I could see what he meant. It was probably true. I had felt a lot less self-conscious at the orthodontists. In the examination room. Of course once I got back to the waiting room, I was already all embarrassed by how I looked....

"Sometimes it was a bit tough," Charles admitted. "Like when I got the headgear. She had the facebow lying there when she changed my wires, so I knew what was coming, but it was so long in coming. And she had a girl come over and watch, and the girl knew what was coming, and you could see the dread in her eyes. And then the orthodontist first tried to see how it fit with me still with the cheek retractor, so I had like no sense of what it was like, but I could see this girl's eyes bulging in reaction. And then the orthodontist took the cheek retractor out, and fit the headgear properly, with the strap. And then she put the mirror on the tray in front of me and she left me to stare at my reflection, and that was pretty hard. You know. Headgear."

I could just imagine the feeling. I had never had headgear, but I remembered sleepless nights worrying about getting it. The idea of what it must then be like to face it still gave me shivers.

"But the visits to the orthodontist really helped," Charles told me. "That total reprieve for an hour or two. That total immersive...almost joy. And it made it easier for me to appreciate the braces when I was by myself. To admit to myself that, hey, these are kind of OK. It's OK to like the feel and ache and sensations of them in my mouth, at least in the privacy of my own place and time.

"But I made another discovery, too, and that really helped too. How I could turn braces to my advantage. Another fleeting consolation that can't really balance out life in braces as a whole but is a nice unexpected positive."

6.

I couldn't imagine a positive side to having braces. Other than the end result, of course. But Charles had a mouthful of metal, plastic, and elastics, and he strapped on a headgear at night, so he obviously wasn't anywhere close to that yet. But, looking both cocky and slightly embarrassed, he grinned through the braces and there was practically a twinkle in his eye. He was sure he was onto something.

"Like I said, that whole last month or two of ninth grade I behaved like everyone expected me to behave and I felt like I expected I should feel, now that I had braces. You know, how everything *seems* to be like always, if you just take a quick look, or reflect on how people act and talk, but if you scratch the surface just a bit then it all looks totally different. You don't behave the same, and people don't treat you the same. Everything is that small bit off – which is enough to make you completely uncertain of everything. And especially of yourself.

"I think it's that way with everyone who has braces. Even though, looking at them, you always think how much better your friends or classmates are handling having them. But deep down they're racked by all the same insecurities."

I nodded.

"Which is exactly what I needed to realize," Charles said triumphantly.

I wasn't so sure how helpful that insight was. I always suspected it, but it never did me much good while I endured my braced period.

Charles began to explain. "Around the end of school one of my classmates is going to have a party. Not a huge blow-out. Pretty select. Like twenty or twenty-five kids. She's invited some tenth graders, too. The girl giving the party is one of the more attractive ones in school. One a lot of the kids look up to or envy.

"We aren't close friends, but we hang out sometimes, and there's sort of some mild flirtation going on. She's been planning the party for a while, and she invited me early on. Before I got the braces. Once I had the braces...well, she didn't talk about the party so much when I was around. Or remind me that I was invited. And any sort of flirtation was now all cold shoulder. The week before she even said, 'If you don't feel like coming, it's OK.' Because...well, let's face it. Braces.

"But my parents know her parents – through work – and I had mentioned I would be going, and I couldn't really back out, because my parents wouldn't forgive me, and it wasn't like I was actually disinvited. And I did want to go, because even though I felt self-conscious about the braces I figured it couldn't be as bad as it was at school, because these were kids I knew better and they hadn't really said too much to my face about the braces....

"Of course, I should have known better. My actual friends were close enough to me to make fun of me to my face, and kids who didn't know me had no problem laughing at me, but this girl giving the party and the crowd she had invited, they were all in that sort of grey zone friendship. Which I knew, but somehow totally missed –

because that grey zone was sort of the most comfortable, now that I had braces. That no-reaction zone. Not rude but also, I realized – too late – not friendly. Of course they talked – behind my back.

"So my mom drops me off at the party and it doesn't take me long to realize what everyone else there also realizes. I am the only one with braces. All that was missing was the flashing neon sign pointing to me. *LOSER*.

"And the girl giving the party is coldly friendly, and everyone else pretends it doesn't matter or they don't notice. But, you know. You can see it in how the small clusters form, and people move closer or further away, and it wasn't like I was this radioactive island everyone avoided, but somehow I always found myself on the periphery. Near the edge. Ready to topple over it.

"In fact, there was somebody else there with braces. The girl who was hosting the party had a younger sister – like two grades behind us. I knew her by sight and name, but little else, but she was there and it turned out she had recently gotten braces too. Of course I avoided her as soon as I noticed, because the only two kids with braces standing together…well, that would only double the focus on what made us different from everyone else. But because I was kind of trying to keep my distance I was also watching her. She had a friend with her, another seventh-grader, a bit taller, a bit more developed. I guess the sisters' parents forced the older one to put up with the younger one, and the younger one brought in a friend to at least keep her some company.

"They sort of hung out by themselves, but they joked around with some of the other kids too. Except you could see that the boys who did talk to them paid more attention to the more mature-looking friend. Who didn't have braces, of course. The girl with the braces was consistently sidelined. Like I was.

"Eventually her friend has to leave, leaving the girl with the braces all alone. And you can see how she doesn't really know what to do with herself, because all alone, with all these older kids she really doesn't fit in, and now she's missing her friend who was sort of able to bridge the age gap. So she's pretty much just standing around nervously and miserably.

"Then it dawns on me. What I can do. So I go up to her and say *Hi* – and 'Pretty hard to fit in, right?'

"She sees my braces, of course, and even though I don't say *because of the braces*, she can read that into my words. She feels I understand. She shrugs and nods – just a bit, because she doesn't really want to admit she doesn't fit in. Maybe not to me, maybe not to herself.

"'Want to go inside?' I ask her. 'Away from all the attention?'

"At least she smiles at that – and it's that kind of smile where you can see she desperately wants to hide what's hidden behind her lips but can't. And she shrugs and agrees and we go into the living room and sit down on the big couch.

"I get right to it. 'So how long have you had the braces?' I know they must be pretty new too, because I hadn't noticed them before and I did see her at school and with her sister sometimes.

"She doesn't really want to talk about it, but she admits, 'Around a month.'

"'I've had them about twice as long,' I sigh. 'And it doesn't seem to get any easier.' We're in the same boat, I'm telling her. And then I smile and say, 'Your sister must be so relieved.' And she looks at me like she doesn't know what I mean.

"'Well you...I mean, I really like your sister, and she's really pretty. *Really* pretty. But the last couple of times I saw you, I mean I couldn't help but think...but realize, well...*wow*. I mean I tried not to pay attention, because I'm friends with your sister and I want to stay friends with her, and you're not even in high school yet, and so I only get occasional glimpses of you. But I'm sure she realizes what's going on. I mean, obviously I'm not the only one who noticed it. She must have seen how other boys started looking at you. Noticing that you're becoming the prettier one. That you're going to be...well, wow. And obviously she can't let on she's jealous of her younger sister, right? So the braces must have come as a big relief to her. Now she doesn't have to worry for a couple of years, right? Now things are back to the natural order. Older sister, younger sister. The boys all pay attention to her, and you….well, they don't think of you in that way, and she doesn't have to worry about them doing so for a couple of years.'

"You could see the whole range of emotions going through her head. She was excited by the thought that maybe people found her pretty and crushed by the thought that now, with the braces, they didn't."

"You were really playing on her insecurities," I interrupted Charles.

"Totally!" he said. Proudly. And he continued in the same vein. "Then I said, 'Maybe it was your sister that convinced the orthodontist to install those kinds of braces,' sort of pointing at her mouth. Then before she had chance to really react, I pretended to walk it back, like I just realized it wasn't a funny joke. 'No,' I said, shaking my head, 'I'm sure the orthodontist determined you really needed braces like that. In order to fix your bite and so on.' Making her feel even worse about what she had in her mouth of course."

"That's kind of mean," I said, even though I found Charles's account fascinating.

"But I was only saying out loud what she was thinking all the time anyway," Charles said. "That's what I realized. Everyone always has this anodyne patter when they talk to you about your braces – I'm sure you got that too. Especially from your parents and relatives and friends, right? *They're not so bad* and *It's not for very long*. But no one comes out and confirms your real fears and worries, about how they see you and what they think of you. The closest to honest anyone will be is when they commiserate about maybe the braces hurting, or how annoying it is when food gets stuck in them. But no one acknowledges what it's like to be smirked about and pitied – like we are everywhere we turn, right?"

I had to agree. Of course he was right about that.

"So I dial it back a bit – but keep harping on the stuff no one else is willing to talk about. 'Have you got used to the way people look at you?' I ask her. 'Or your friends, how they pretend it doesn't matter you have braces, but you can tell how they're a bit embarrassed to be around you now. Especially in public.'

"And the girl is lapping it up. Because someone is finally sharing her worst fears about having braces. Everything she's been feeling since she got them, but which everyone has tried to negate or ignore.

"And of course I bring it back to boys. I say, 'Maybe it's better this way. It gives you a chance to grow up without constantly having to deal with all those boys slobbering over you. Like your sister does,' I rub it in.

"I tell her, 'I mean, I saw you with your friend earlier, how some of the ninth and tenth graders were buzzing around her. She's probably not really ready to deal with that yet, right? And with the braces you don't really have to worry. You'll know that if any boy pays attention to you, it's really because of *you*. Not the stuff that's basically on the mind of boys your – or my – age, ninety-five percent of the time....'

"You see how I was pretending to see the positive – while actually just confirming all her worst fears, right? That with the braces she was undesirable. Untouchable."

"I see it all too clearly," I said. Though I couldn't wipe the smile off my face at his deviousness.

"I take my chances and add, 'At least you got your first kiss out of the way, before you got the braces, right?' I figure I can spin it either way, regardless whether she has or not.

"She actually shakes her head embarrassedly. 'Not really,' she admits, in barely a whisper. I pretend to look *really* surprised. How a girl like her could not have had some of that experience. And then I pretend like it's OK – making sure that she can tell I am pretending.... I tell her, 'Well that's probably better anyway. This way you don't know what you're missing. There won't be that huge, yawning, longing gap between first kisses and next kiss, because you're still working your way up to…. And, like I said, it probably is better to be more mature and grown-up before you start in on all that romantic and intimate stuff.'

"She looks doubtful and dejected. And I pretend to notice, and say, overly cheerfully, 'It probably just seems like forever now. But it's not that long. You have the braces for a year or two, so you're kind of out of commission, but then they come off – well, there are a few months in retainers, and maybe a little more time so that the boys can forget that you were *that girl with braces*…. But at some point, in a couple of years…well, your sister won't be able to hold a candle to you.' And I smile at her – trying not to show my braces – like I was giving her the best news ever.

"Of course that's not how she sees it. Basically, I've told her she's an unkissable ugly duckling for like the next three years. Which she of course has been imagining for the past month anyway – but no one has ever come right out and spelled it out so clearly. I'm not telling her anything she hasn't thought a million times herself, but it's still a devastating blow to actually hear it.

"She's really depressed now, but finally she asks, 'What about you? You're in high school already. Isn't that even worse?'

"She's hoping for some company in her misery. It doesn't really help – I'm a boy, I'm so much older, it can't really make her feel any better if I'm suffering too – but at least she's not the only one. So of course instead of telling her what she expects to hear – I lie.

"I pretend to be embarrassed to have to admit it. I make a face like I'm reluctant to tell her. Finally I sheepishly admit, 'It's unfair, isn't it?' And she's wondering *What?* But I take my time in explaining. 'It probably makes a difference that I'm a boy,' I tell her. 'And that I'm older. It's a different situation.' And she's wondering what's different about it.

"I admit the obvious. I have to. 'Of course no girl wants to be seen with someone outfitted with things like these,' I say, pointing at and revealing my braces. And she looks almost relieved that I confirm that. 'So it's not like I'm going to have a girlfriend, or a girl is even going to go out with me. I mean, like your sister – she's probably making a face that I'm even here, because even that is too close an association with someone with braces, right?'

"She understands that. She nods. Her sister has probably made exactly that kind of face about her, now that she has braces.

"'But the thing is,' I say, 'a lot of girls, by the time they're around my age, they've already experienced a lot. They've kissed and been kissed by a couple of boys. Maybe had boyfriends. Maybe gotten more serious with some boys, right?' All things this girl has been dreaming of but knows are now out of her braced reach.... 'And these girls...,' I say, trying to sound even more embarrassed about what I was admitting, 'they're curious. They've kissed normal boys. But someone with braces? That's different. Intriguing. That's something they'll never be able to try again, not once they're out of high school.... And as long as no one knows, as long as they experiment in secret....'

"So the girl's eyes go all wide. 'So you've kissed girls with your braces?' And I pretend to be embarrassed about it, but I nod. 'Just a few, of course. I couldn't believe it at first. I was amazed how...curious some were. I thought the braces would shut that part of my life down completely, but instead I find *more* girls coming up to me. When they're sure no one's watching. It's weird, because it's not like they'd go out with me – some of them even practically pretend they don't know me if I see them in public. But alone...they like it. Or at least like trying it.'

"She looked totally dumbfounded. 'It's not like braces make it physically impossible to kiss, right?' I remind her. 'You just have to be a little more careful. And in a way...there are more sensations there, I guess. The girls...they like it. The different texture, I guess. Maybe even the elastics?' I laugh. 'I mean, I have no idea how it is for them – I've never kissed a girl with braces. But they really, really seem to like it.' I pretend to be just as amazed by that as anyone else would be.

"'So,' I conclude, 'completely out of the blue, the braces have sort of enhanced my love life. In a weird way, because I think anyone of these girls would rather die than admit to having done anything like that with me, and so it's not like I can call one up to go to the movies on a Friday night. But in that intimate way....'

"The girl looked stunned and in awe. And I look at her and pretend to realize I may have said too much. Revealing that we aren't in the same boat after all, but that she's been left behind even by someone who has such an awful set of braces. 'But it's really...not that special,' I try to tell her. 'It's kind of shallow, right? Only physical. So you're probably better off, that that doesn't come up for you. That you have to...that you *can* wait."

"Of course now she feels it's even more unfair that she has to wait. She feels she's singled out even more. But she also sees an opportunity.... She even thinks she's really being sly when she then asks me, 'You really think I'm pretty?'

"And I make that golly gee expression, arching my eyebrows like *Could there be any doubt?* And she is pretty. I mean, she's still a kid, and she can't compare to her sister, who is a real knock out, but she is pretty. And even with the self-doubts every girl seems to have about their own looks, she's willing to believe that someone could find her pretty.

"I tell her, like it's the most obvious thing in the world. 'Come on, anyone who glimpses you – they do a double-take, right? I mean, my God....'

"She senses a *but*, but I don't say it. I leave it hanging out there, until she looks sadly into her lap and speaks aloud what she imagines we – and the whole world – are thinking. 'But the braces....'

"I don't even try to deny it. I act like that's even more obvious than her beauty. 'Well, yeah,' I stutter. 'But that's only temporary. A detour, right?' I pretend to be looking for a good spin on it – making sure she realizes there isn't one.

"She's bottomed out now. Sees her situation is hopeless. But she thinks maybe the door is open just the tiniest crack.... She barely dares look up from her lap, but she forces herself to, looking me in the eyes and asking, 'Have you ever wanted to kiss a girl with braces?'

"At first I don't take the hint and answer like I would any question. 'I guess I've been sort of curious...,' and then I pretend to catch myself, like I just realized what she means She looks at me pleadingly, and I look her deep in the eyes. I reach forward and brush her cheek with the back of my hand."

Charles reaches forward and does the same to mine to demonstrate. I'm listening to him, rapt. I feel my frustrating retainers in my mouth, and I remember what it was like to have braces, and I can imagine exactly what that poor girl was feeling, and all her desperation. I was listening with bated breath, eagerly hoping that he gave her at least that small satisfaction....

But he didn't make it easy for her.

"I stare her in the eyes," Charles continues, and I say, 'But would that even be fair? To you? To you sister? Don't you want all that to happen with a boy who can give you more than just one kiss? And don't you want it to be with a boy who doesn't have braces? Don't you want to wait until neither of you have braces?'

"And she is almost quivering with hope. She just shakes her head – barely moving it, because she doesn't want to break that eye contact, that deep mutual gaze, as I seem to be looking into her soul."

And as he's talking Charles is gazing just as deeply into my eyes, and I can barely breathe with anticipation.

"I wait. I make her wait. Like I'm making the hardest decision. And then I slowly lean forward, and she closes her eyes and leans forward too and puckers her lips expectantly, and mine meet hers and we sink into this long, cautious, beautiful kiss.

"And I had kissed some girls before – not with my braces, but before – and it was nice, even hot, but this was something different and more. Maybe because she was so desperate, so ready, giving herself fully into nothing but the moment. And maybe because we had to be careful because of the braces, so it wasn't like simple wild abandon.

"And we just lost ourselves in each other. She even took my hand and pulled it up to her breast, so I would cup it, knead it, hold it, and even though she was still pretty young she was already well-developed but still not really full grown, not there, not that way, not like her sister. But it still felt good and right."

I couldn't help it, but I sighed out loud as Charles described it. Like I did at the romantic happy end of a really good movie. It was so satisfying. Even as it left me with my own unfulfilled sense of longing....

"And when we finally separated, her eyes glistening, her smile beaming, she looked like she had known the greatest happiness in her life. I let her soak it in some, the feeling, sitting there with her, and then I was saved by the bell – the buzz of my phone, as Mom texted me that she was on her way to pick me up. So that helped spare us some of the post-kiss awkwardness.

"Getting up, I told her, 'You're going to be OK. You're going to be fine. And that next boy you kiss, after you got your braces off, he's a going to be a very lucky guy, because you're a very special girl. And you'll be so unbelievably beautiful.

"She blushed and smiled. She didn't even flinch when I suggested the next kiss would only come after her braces were off. She was probably even OK with it. At least she had had the experience. It would hold her over for a long time.

"I told her, 'That was something very special for me too.' All she could do was smile – the smile still bursting off her face – and wave goodbye. She was still speechless. But happy, I think."

I wasn't sure how I felt about Charles's story. On the one hand it was heartwarming and romantic. But it was also like he took advantage of the girl. I asked him whether he felt bad about it.

"Maybe a tiny pang of my conscience," he admitted. "But mainly because she was so young. Not that young, but like two years younger than me, so that felt a bit...improper. But otherwise? I gave her everything she could have dreamed of. Sure, I manipulated her into it – but I can't imagine anything could have made her happier than how things wound up."

"But you reinforced all her terrible worries about her braces."

"Didn't I just bring them out into the open? Address them honestly – which no one else does. Sure, it hurts. It's a burden. But it's also a relief – to know you're not the only one who understands. To hear someone else say all this." He looked at me with that penetrating gaze. "Wouldn't you have liked a boy to tell those truths to you when you had braces?"

I tried not to show any emotion or reaction. Because of course he was right. If he had used those lines on insecure me when I had braces, I would have desperately wanted to melt in his arms too.

Worse, part of me felt those very same urges right now....

7.

Charles looked pleased with himself. "Of course, once I saw how easily this worked, I had to try it some more. And the amazing thing is, if you're patient and show empathy and you're honest – brutally honest, but honest – about what it means to have braces, the girls fall for it. Or maybe it's not amazing at all – it makes perfect sense.

"Braces magnify your insecurities exponentially, right? Everyone tiptoes around that, and them. But by diving right in, by confronting them, the girls feel I understand."

"So you go around seducing girls with braces?"

"It's not like that. Not totally. Sometimes, with some of them I really do just talk. They like that. They need that. I don't...force myself on any girl that isn't ready for it. And some of them aren't. Even some girls my age, they're just not ready for anything – for them it really can be good to have the braces as an excuse to avoid dealing with that kind of thing."

"But others?"

Charles looked sheepish. "Sure, I guess I take advantage. But I do think it gives them something too."

"And this always works?"

"Of course not. It's not like some magic potion, or spell. Well, maybe it would, if I really put my heart into it. I think it might. But I pick and choose, and sometimes the situation just isn't right. Girls who have had braces for a while, they're usually too hardened. They've built up this shell, and that's really tough to penetrate. The easiest ones are those who have just gotten them. Who are a month or two into their treatment – enough time for it all to sink in, just what has happened to them, but not enough for them to have put up all those barriers to feeling anything.

"Twice I heard about girls who were going to get braces, so I could lay the groundwork beforehand. That was even better. Help guide them, as they transition from being normal kids to braced kids."

It sounded awful, but he was right, wasn't he? I could have used some guidance when I suddenly found myself braced, and found that it was so much more, and in such different ways, than anyone had let me expect.

"But you don't have like relationships with these girls, right?" I asked him.

"No," he admitted. "It's pretty much only physical. And spiritual, in a way. Going over common ground in a way no one ever has with them. A short union of minds, and feelings..."

"And mouths," I completed the thought for him.

He laughed. "Something like that. Sometimes. But they don't really want more. Or expect more. I mean, I certainly don't encourage the idea of the possibility of a relationship. I guess, I try to undermine it, as much as I can. But I think they agree, that kids who both have braces going out...it's too ridiculous.

"The moments of encouragement and support – that seems to be enough for them."

"Don't you want more?" I asked him.

Charles shrugged. "Sometimes I think about it. Not in the moment, but after the moment. But honestly, I believe what I tell them. That it's not really realistic to be in a relationship when you have braces. Relationships in junior high or high school are awkward and weird enough. Throw in braces...who needs that?"

I nodded. I couldn't have imagined having a boyfriend – even one without braces – when I had mine. But I was younger than he was now when I had braces.

"So you're constantly scouting for girls in braces?" I asked him. Partially as a joke – but I was curious.

"Not scouting. But I keep my eyes open. Like all kids do about kids of the other sex, right? It just narrows it down. But the funny thing is, after I told the girl that some older, more experienced girls who didn't have braces were curious...well, I decided to see if that might work too. And it does!"

"Come on...," I said in disbelief.

"No, really. It's a good line. Obviously it doesn't work all the time. I mean, mostly I strike out – but it's better than any other line I have to offer any normal girl. I mean, honestly, it's pretty much my only option. And some girls really are curious, and they get that it's like an unusual opportunity, so why not take advantage.

"I mean, I'd never try it with the girls at school. But I travel a lot with my parents, and they drag me to parties with people I'll never see again, and usually there are bored teenage girls there too. So I give them my pitch. The worst that can happen is they laugh in my face – and since that sometimes happens when I just open my mouth and reveal the braces, why not try?"

I had to ask. "Is that what you're doing with me? Making your pitch?" Part of me liked the idea. Of the attention, the interest, the effort.

He laughed, revealing his braces – reminding me of his braces – and leaned a bit closer. "Aren't you curious what it would be like to kiss someone with braces?" he said in a seductive tone.

I flinched, thinking that he was really going to lean in and kiss me, but he just laughed at my reaction and pulled back. He didn't seem disappointed. In fact, it didn't seem he had planned on kissing me at all, which almost disappointed me.

"I can't really imagine kissing someone with braces," I said, still a bit flustered.

He shrugged. "But part of you must be curious. About what it feels like. The different sensations. Not necessarily me, but in the abstract – you must be curious."

I kind of felt backed in a corner, forced to admit that he was right. But I couldn't figure out what he was after. Or if he was after anything. Part of me wanted him to be trying to seduce me, but he didn't seem to be. Except for those flashes when he did. I thought about his story, how subtly he manipulated that poor girl. Was he working a similar game one me?

"Do you just make out with the girls?" I asked him. Changing the subject without changing the subject....

He shrugged. "Not just. Usually, sure. But some want more. Sometimes it works out that more is possible."

"So you've slept with some of these girls?"

He nodded like it was perfectly natural. "A few."

Kissing with braces. Making love with braces. It was so hard to imagine. Of course, I had been younger when I had mine. But what girl would sleep with a boy with braces? Though looking at him, and having spent the day with him, I couldn't deny that I was strongly drawn to everything else about him. That, if he hadn't had braces, if I hadn't seen him in headgear…I'd want nothing more than to get closer to him. It was mesmerizing listening to him talk – I was a totally captive audience – and I really felt a connection on that plane. If not for the glint of the metal between his lips, and the lisp, I'd want that connection to extend and expand in the physical. The deeply physical, I sighed to myself.

I guess part of me was also a bit relieved that that scenario was purely hypothetical. I had never slept with a boy. Never really come close to it – and now this proximity unsettled me. I had made out with a few boys, and funnily, this goofing around with Charles, this banter, seemed closer to sex than anything had with those boys, even when they were slobbering over me and groping me.

I guess the braces, and the stupid retainers I was still wearing were proving to be useful fencing separating us. Insuring that things wouldn't slip into any uncharted – at least by me – territories.

8.

"How much longer are you going to have them?" I asked. Mom had said something about how he was supposed to get them off after like a year but the orthodontist was making him wear them longer. Even he had said something about only needing them for a year or something.

Charles gazed in my eyes again, and I had to keep myself from showing any emotion because he really had such a strong, penetrating stare. It was like he was evaluating me. Whether I was worthy of his confidence. Or even just his time. And also like he was gazing into my soul.

"Promise not to tell anyone?" he said.
"What?"
"What I want to tell you."
"What's the big secret?"
"It's not…well, it is sort of a secret. Mostly, it's sort of embarrassing. Like I'd rather my parents didn't…fully understand. Because they wouldn't really understand."

He was embarrassed that the orthodontist didn't trust him to wear his retainers and was keeping him in braces for that reason? I could understand that he was ashamed of that – though I didn't want to burst his bubble, but since Mom told me, his mom was obviously already fully in that picture. But I nodded understandingly and said, "Sure, mums the word."

"You don't tell anyone, OK?" he said, looking very serious.

"OK," I agreed. Who was I going to tell? I hadn't told my friends about him yet, and even if I eventually did, braces gossip was hardly what I was eager to share.

He nodded, accepting that I meant it. "OK," he said. I think he even sort of took a breath. Like he was preparing himself to say something difficult. It was the first glimpse of something other than the confident, secure boy he had been for the past two days.

"Having braces is a pain," Charles said. "Not so much a physical pain – there's that, but I didn't find that too much of a problem. But, you know, the whole facing the world with these problem. That's a pain."

I nodded. I remembered it well enough. And at his age it must have been even worse.

"So a few months ago I was finishing up tenth grade, and I was thinking about what lay ahead. The braces were set to come off soon, but then I'd get retainers. And Mom had already talked that over with the orthodontist, and the orthodontist told her she only used the kind you have, with the wires across the teeth. And I guess I probably wouldn't have to wear those for long, 24/7, but for at least part of eleventh grade....

"And though the wiring looks OK on most girls – or great on some," he smiled at me, "it's not a great man-look. Or boy-look. So as I began to think about it I realized even finishing with braces, I wouldn't really be getting past them. A few months going around with that silver smile you're now sporting. And even after that, everyone would remember me having had braces. Like I told that girl at the party – people don't forget something like that fast. Girls, I realized, wouldn't forget.

"And when I thought about it, I realized I had a pretty good thing going the way things were. No girlfriend potential – but that seemed out of reach post-braces, too. At least at high school, where everyone knows me, and wouldn't be able to get that deeply embedded braced image of me like this out of their minds. But otherwise, I was doing OK with the girls. I was having some fun. Getting some satisfaction. And even providing actual support to a lot of them who don't get it elsewhere, which kind of made me feel good too. Like I was helping them, which I think I was.

"Once the braces came off, my approach would be much harder to pull off. I'd probably come across more as creepy than helpful, right? As long as I had braces, it was easy for a girl to trust and believe me. Once they were off, I could still press the same buttons, but it wouldn't sound as convincing. And it would be much harder just to initiate that contact.

"The other thing I realized was that I didn't mind having the braces. I mean, of course I minded, like everyone who has them does, because they interfere with a lot of everyday stuff and because in public you look like...this. But on balance I didn't mind. I liked the feel of them in my mouth. Even the headgear – as long as no one saw me wearing it. And honestly, the intimate stuff, the kissing – the braces sort of forced and added tenderness to it, and I liked that too. I liked having the braces when I kissed a girl, whether she had them or not.

"So at my next orthodontist appointment – this was around May, when I had had the braces for about a year – when I was strapped down in the chair and the orthodontist came over to start working on me I told her I wanted to speak with her. Afterwards, in her office, in private. About my braces. 'You can't tell me here?' she asked, but I told her I'd really rather talk in her office. Face to face, too – not with me lying there and her towering over me!

"So she nods and begins with the usual routine and gets around to rewiring me. And has her assistant bring over some kid to show me off as an example again. And when she's finished she tells the assistant who starts cleaning up and unstrapping my wrists, 'Bring him to my office when you're done.' And she smiles at me and tells me she'll be there soon.

"So the assistant leads me to the office, and I sit there nervously waiting. Finally the orthodontist comes in and sits behind her desk and smiles. I think she expects the usual sort of plea or complaint. *Can't they come off sooner?* or something like that. She even smiles to herself as if I'm confirming it when the first thing I say is, 'So my braces are supposed to come off pretty soon, right?'

"She leans back and says typically noncommittally, 'We're making good progress, but we shouldn't get ahead of ourselves.'

"She looks a bit surprised when I don't press her on that and instead say, 'And I'm going to get retainers after that? The kind with the wires?'

"'Hawley retainers,' she says. 'Fulltime for a few months.'

"I remind her of my history of not wearing my retainers. And I tell her, 'I'm worried about being able to handle that.' And before she has a chance to say whatever she wants to say about that, I say, 'So I was thinking, maybe you could leave the braces on longer? So that they're like the retainers. Holding everything in place.'

"She looks really surprised. 'No one ever asks me to let them wear their braces *longer*,' she says.

"'But it's possible, right?' I ask. 'It would work, wouldn't it?'

"She thinks it over and then says it would. 'But it's an extreme solution.'

"'But I don't really mind the braces that much,' I tell her. 'I think they must be easier to deal with than the retainers. And I just don't trust myself with anything I could take out.'

"She reminds me that I've been wearing my headgear like I'm supposed to, but I tell her that's different. I never have to wear it in public. And it's headgear – it's not as uncomfortable as the retainers.

"She leans forward as all this begins to sink in and looks at me in kind of disbelief. 'And you'd really rather continue to wear the braces?'

"And I try to make clear with my expression that that is absolutely my preference. 'I really think it would be much easier. And I don't mind if it's for longer – you know, however long it takes the teeth to really be set in place.'

"'You'd still need retainers afterwards, at least at night,' she reminds me.

"I nod. 'Right. And actually I was thinking, with the braces still on you could maybe make sort of a practice retainer for me to wear. Even to wire it in, so I can get used to it. Have to get used to it.'

"I can tell she's intrigued by the idea. 'But if the braces are functioning as the retainer, we'd have to leave them in quite a while longer,' she's thinking out loud.

"I assure her. 'That's really no problem. Even better – keep them on until we're absolutely sure everything is totally secured in place. I know so many kids in school, even when they wear their retainers like their orthodontists tell them to, there's usually some drift or tension, unless they're wearing their retainers all the time.'

"I even add. 'I mean, I'd like to get them off by the time I graduate from high school, but anything until then I'd be more or less fine with.'

"She's surprised. She hadn't been thinking of that time frame. 'That's almost two more years,' she reminds me.

"I shrug, like it's no big deal at all. Even though my heart is racing, because it is a pretty scary idea.

"She leans back and nods to herself, thinking it over. 'You really are prepared to do this?' she asks. I have to keep myself from nodding too enthusiastically, or adding *Please*.

"Finally she says, 'Let me think about it. I have some concerns about unnecessarily keeping them on. The effects on your oral hygiene – though you take good care of your teeth. Let me think about it, and we'll see next time you come in.

"I'm kind of disappointed that she doesn't immediately agree, but at least there's some hope. I do ask her not to tell my mom. Not like this anyway. 'I think it would be better if she believes it's necessary, rather than my…our choice.'

"'You want me to lie to your mother?' she asks.

"'It's more a white lie, right?' I argue. 'As long as in your professional opinion it's OK, and it's something I think is the better course of action – and I'm the patient …. Telling her it's our choice would just confuse her.'

"She didn't say she wouldn't tell Mom, but she smiled and nodded.

"So then I had to wait another five weeks until my next appointment. I made sure to *really* brush and floss, to make sure my gums were totally healthy – I could see how she could be worried about the braces staying on affecting my oral health. Otherwise there wasn't much I could do. Except wonder whether this was really what I wanted to do.

"But I consoled another girl who had just gotten her braces during that time, and when I did that I didn't have any doubts any longer. The braces were gold. I didn't want to miss the opportunities they opened up for me. So I had to hope the orthodontist would see it my way.

"Finally Mom takes me to my next appointment. The assistant gets me ready in the chair and straps my wrists down. The orthodontist finally comes over and sits on the stool beside me and turns on the spotlight.

"'So how are we doing, Charles?' she asks.

"And my voice is trembling when I say, 'Well.'

"She peers around in my mouth a bit, and then she sits back upright again. 'So what you suggested last time, is that really something you want to consider?'

"I nod. Nod really hard.

"'You know that we could be taking these off in a few months?' she tells me. 'You could be braces-free around the start of school in the fall. Wearing retainers, but braces-free.'

"Braces-free. That's a lot to dangle in front of anyone who has them. But I know what I want. 'No,' I say. 'It's better if I continue to have them.'

"'It would make an interesting case study,' she says. And I can see that she is curious about it. 'Retention is an interesting and problematic issue, and leaving braces on as retainers hasn't been widely explored. If you're really willing....'

"I nod again.

"'But to really be sure, we would have to keep the braces on until well into your senior year,' she tells me, looking like she's worried that that's a deal breaker.

"'I'd really rather start college without braces,' I tell her. 'But until then, I'm totally fine with having them.'

"She bites her lip, like she can't believe she's actually considering doing this to a patient. But then she says, 'OK.'

"And I break out in the biggest smile and thank her. It's the best news I've had in longer than I can remember. I can't believe it is – *you get to keep your braces!* does not sound like good news. But it was exactly what I wanted to hear.

"Even when she put the cheek retractor in, it felt like that grin was still on my face. 'You're sure?' she asked again before she wired in the new archwires. And I nodded. And she said, 'Because if we're going this route, then we'll be making some adjustments to your treatment. Slowing down the process, too.'

"It's a small shock then, to realize that this is real, but I nod again, and she begins installing the archwire. And when she's finished and fits the headgear again she tells me that she's adjusting that too, so the pull isn't quite as strong.

"When she's done she tells me, 'Well, I guess I should talk to your mother.'

"I panic a bit. 'You're not going to tell her, are you?'

"But she doesn't answer. And I understand that she has to tell her something.

"When the assistant comes to clean me up and unstrap me I ask to her wait a while. 'The orthodontist said she's going to talk to my mom,' I tell her. 'Could you leave me here until they're done, so I don't have to wait in the waiting room?'

"She does, and then like ten minutes later she comes and releases me, and I go to the waiting room, where Mom is looking grim but stoical. She doesn't say anything right away, and we get the appointment slip for next time and leave.

"On the drive home she finally asks me, 'Did the orthodontist talk to you about your braces?'

"I pretend to be clueless and shrug. 'Just the usual. Why?'

"Mom gets the way she does when she has to break bad news. 'Well, she called me into her office and...well, you know how you were only supposed to have them for...well, not too much longer? Well, she says that they're going to have to stay on longer after all.' Mom glanced at me quickly, worried how I must be taking this horrible news. 'You're not too disappointed, are you?'

"I try to hide my relief. 'It's OK, Mom,' I tell her. 'It's more important to get it right, right? They're not that bad.'

"She can barely not wince when I say *They're not that bad*, but she gives me that *What a good boy* smile – with a lot of that *You poor thing!* smile to it – and even pats me on the leg.

"I realize I am supposed to show a bit of concern, so I ask her, 'How much longer?'

"Mom looks at me quickly all pityingly. 'Let's not worry about that for now,' she says. And from the tone of her voice you'd swear that what she meant was *Forever*. I felt bad how disappointed she was. And relieved that this was happening. And scared to death, too."

9.

"So you're telling me you don't actually need to have those braces right now?" I asked Charles incredulously.

He had that abashed look. "Maybe. She'd have taken them off sometime around now, probably. But I'd have retainers like yours, fulltime."

"But still...."

"Are those so much better than these?" he asked, pointing to my teeth and then his.

"Maybe not. But it's like such a huge step. They're removable..."

"Which would have been a problem," he reminded me.

"...and they're the final step. Except at night – but no one really has to know about that."

He shrugged. "So far, I'm not sorry. The benefits outweigh the drawbacks. I'm getting more out of them than I would if I had moved on."

"Seriously?"

"Like this time I'm spending with you. If I were already in retainers – no way you wouldn't find that even more gross than me with these." He bared his braces again. "No way would you have agreed to wear yours while we hung out. So we wouldn't have hung out the same way. See?"

I wasn't convinced. "And so you're going to have them for another two years?"

He shrugged and smiled. "Not that long. I think she'll take them off sometime my senior year, like before graduation. But she says I have to leave it in her hands, to decide when the time is right. Which I don't mind doing."

I shook my head in disbelief. And a little bit of admiration.

"The only slightly scary thing is that she is making me get used to the retainers. So she's wired in this training set to start, but she says she's going to replace them with progressively larger ones. And these already affect my speech so much. Like yours do. So I'm kind of worried about what it will it be like when they're two or three sizes larger."

I peered more closely. I had suspected but not really been sure. "So you have like an upper retainer?"

"Yeah," he said, opening his mouth wider so I could see. "Do you want to feel?" he asked, opening his mouth again.

"What?"

"With your finger. Aren't you curious?"

I kind of was. Especially now that he said it. But it seemed like such a strange thing to do. My friends were all so guarded about what was in their mouths when they had braces. No one invited me to touch. They barely wanted anyone to look....

"Go ahead," he said, opening his mouth wide and leaning his head back a bit.

It was hard to resist. So I slowly moved my index finger to his mouth, then turned it upward and let the tip slide across the smooth, rounded plastic. I sort of expected him to close his mouth around it, teasingly pretending to bite it. Or to suck on it. But he sat there patiently as I rubbed my fingertip across the surfaces.

It wasn't any different than feeling my own retainers, which I had done before – and did constantly, with my tongue – and yet it felt much more stirring. Intimate, but in an entirely different way from what I was used to. Sexy, even.

"So you want to feel mine now?" I asked. It seemed right to make the reciprocal offer.

He did turn so he was facing closer to me, but he smiled and shook his head. "That's OK. Enough girls have already allowed me to explore their orthodontia."

It was weird to realize that I was almost disappointed. That a boy in braces was turning down the opportunity to stick his finger in my mouth.... Something I would have never thought I could be disappointed about.

He stared at me. Looking deep into my eyes. "So what do you think?"

"About what?"

"Everything," he smiled. "My braces experiences."

"It's all…unbelievable. Unusual. Hard to take in."

One of his elbows rested on the back of the couch. One leg was bent between us, almost touching mine. I realized I had lost track of time, and most of space. It was like I was in a bubble with him – a bubble that was getting smaller and smaller, pushing us closer together. I hadn't had this much fun just being with someone…that I could ever recall.

He was just comfortable to be with. With my girlfriends, even my closest ones, there was always an undercurrent of jealousy and competition – sometimes slight, sometimes raging. With boys there was always an awkwardness. With Charles, everything was different. Safe but also irreverent.

The retainers made a difference, too. Left me feeling vulnerable – like the braced girls he talked about. Braces hold you back, even when you try to be outgoing. Retainers too. In the front of my mouth, they remained constantly in the back of my mind, with every word and movement. I couldn't hide them. But it was OK. Because his mouthful was worse than mine, and because he really seemed to appreciate that I was wearing them. Making that sacrifice. And he understood how much of a sacrifice it was.

I realized neither of us had said anything for a while. We'd just been staring into each other's eyes as all these thoughts were running through my head.

He leaned ever so slightly closer, and said ever so slightly more softly, "So aren't you curious what it's like to kiss someone with braces?"

And I smiled, because at that moment there was nothing I wanted to know or do more. All this had built up to this moment, and I smiled my broadest smile, forgetting what I looked like with my retainers, forgetting I had my retainers, and I slowly leaned towards him, and he moved towards me, and our lips met halfway and we melted into one another.

First my lips pressed against his. Soft and moist, but not wet. Then his lips parted slightly and I could feel the metal covering his teeth, the rough, patterned smoothness of the wired brackets, and then more as I kissed him more intently. Then my tongue slid across the wonderful metal, along the elastics, and in, towards the retainer I had just felt with my finger. And his tongue darted into my mouth, and sought out the smooth surfaces of my retainers, and we kissed and we kissed.

It was magical. My previous kisses had been OK, mostly. But my mind always raced along with them. *Was I doing it right? Was he? Wasn't he slobbering too much? Did he have to have that beer? Did my breath taste as badly of beer?*

This sensation was entirely mindless. Beyond thought. Simply all feeling.

We lost ourselves in each other. A wave of actual euphoria went through me.

Gasping, smiling, we briefly unlocked our lips and looked each other in the eyes, all happiness. And lust.

I couldn't resist. I couldn't bear it. I wanted to experience him completely – and so I reached for my mouth and popped out my top retainer. Trying to slip the purple plastic, glistening from my spit, somewhat discreetly away.

Not very successfully, from the way Charles followed my actions, smiling. He titled his head a bit questioningly. He didn't exactly frown – he was still smiling – but he said, "Now you've broken the spell."

I tried to make myself sound seductive as I said, "Wouldn't you rather kiss a girl without these things?" I only briefly held up the retainer. That couldn't look appetizing.

"Maybe. Sometimes. Not here and now," he said, still holding me. "They're…necessary."

I saw that he somehow meant it, and I clicked the warm, wet retainer back in my mouth. It's not like I minded it that much – I minded it less in front of him than when I was by myself – but it seemed a sort of excess layer. And weight. But it was OK wearing it.

"But it's probably better that you broke the spell," he said – rather than leaning back into me and returning to the kissing....

"You should think about what you want," he said. "From me. With me."

"I know what I want," I told him, leaning forward and kissing him again. He didn't recoil, but he had his head pulled uncomfortably far back and returned the kisses lightly.

I pulled back.

"Think about it," he repeated. "Besides, we should probably get some dinner. Aren't you hungry? And the moms will be back before too long."

Dinner? My appetite was still for something very different. How could he have so much self-control? He must have felt that I was ready to give myself completely to him – didn't he want that? Or did he just want me to be sure about that?

OK, he was right that it was getting late. If we started anything now, there was the danger of our moms walking in on us. Though given how I felt – I could feel the moisture oozing out of me in anticipation – I was itching for even the just the roughest, quickest slam banging. A matter of minutes would have sealed the deal for me.

10.

Charles dialed it back almost instantly. While I still tottered lust-drunk he stood up perfectly sober. Even the bulge in his pants was almost gone.

"Dinner?" he suggested, and though it took me a few seconds to adjust my bearings I finally nodded and stumbled after him.

"You might as well take the retainers out now," he said. Sounding sad about it. I wasn't sure it was because he missed the look of them on my teeth, or because for him it sealed our decision, to back away from any further intimacy.

But he was right. Dinner. The moms. The retainers had to go. I went to rinse them off quickly in the bathroom, and then stored them away. I was dizzy and numb as I went through these familiar motions. Both from the high of what we had done and now this low of not seeing it all the way through.

I still found it hard to accept that he could turn it off so quickly. Because of one single lapse – if that's what you could call me taking my retainer out.

As we sat down to eat the food we'd heated up I had to ask him *Why?* again. "Didn't you want to…continue."

He smiled and leaned over his plate and looked me deep in my eyes again. "*Very* much," he said.

I was even more confused. "But I take out my retainer for a moment and you're backing off?"

"Everything in its proper place and time," he said. "I think we…I think you need, or should take the time to think about it. It's better we took a step back."

"There's not much thinking to it, is there?"

He laughed. "No. But getting closer to you means a lot to me, and I don't want to treat you unfairly. Leave you feeling you've been taken advantage of. Sweet-talked by the guy with the braces. I want to be honest. I think it's important to be honest. I can't be there for you, afterwards, for example – by tomorrow night I'll be flying away at a couple of hundred miles an hour. There's no future there, there's just the present. So you have to decide whether or not you want that present, without any possibility of any sort of afterwards."

It was thoughtful – but maybe he was overthinking things? At least I bit my tongue and didn't lamely suggest email, texts, or Snapchat….

"And do you want it to be like this?" he continued. "I don't know how close you've been with other boys, but do you want to get that close to me? There's no getting around my braces, for example. And I won't let you get around your retainers."

I shrugged kind of helplessly. Of course in my fantasies I didn't want my first man to have braces. I could still barely even imagine kissing anyone with braces – even though as he sat across from me I felt that urge rise in me all over again. And I didn't want to even admit – to myself or anyone – that I still had retainers, much less to put them in, in front of him or anyone. Even if he appreciated them. Even if he liked me in them….

He wanted me to think about it, but all I could do was feel a slow boil all over inside me. I felt flush, inside and out.

He calmly helped with the dishes, like everything was normal. Meanwhile I was on a rollercoaster of emotions and sensations.

He went to brush his teeth – and came back wearing his headgear!

"Really?" I said, smiling but genuinely surprised. "The headgear?"

"I told you. I want to be honest with you Totally upfront. Expose myself completely. And I can't expose myself any more than by having this on."

I stared incredulously. And was surprised by how much I still wanted him to kiss me.

"Like when you wear your retainers," he said. "That small chink in the armor that opens you up, that makes you real, that takes all your incredible beauty and magnifies it infinitely."

I blushed. It sounded silly, but I still blushed. I think the only person who had ever said anything positive about my retainers was my orthodontist when she first fit me with them. But even that was just the obligatory professional *Well that looks great!* wasn't it? Even Mom and Dad hadn't been able to hide their disappointment when they saw me with the wires across my teeth, even my friends had shook their heads in pity. *Well they're not **that** bad* was about the best anyone could muster.

But Charles *liked* them. I sometimes liked them, when I looked at myself in the mirror. When I no longer had to wear them out in public, during the day. The simple elegance of the silver wires – I did like that. But I could never admit it, because everyone was so relieved I didn't have to wear them out for anyone to see any longer.

There was the feel of the plastic too. That was often comforting at night in bed – something more I could never admit. But for Charles, it was OK. That was a good feeling.

"The headgear, of course doesn't work like that," He admitted. "But given my braces any hopes that anything about them could be attractive – much less enticing or seductive...."

I bit my lip. He was right, of course. They were awful, and the headgear was ridiculous. Yet in that moment, there, I found him irresistible. Despite the braces. Or, I guess, also because of them. There was something to that whole baring your soul by baring your braces concept. He showed me something of himself – a lot – that no boy had ever shown me, and that made the biggest difference....

We sat down in front of the TV again. On the couch. Close but with a definite space between us. We both realized we needed to be just out of immediate reach of each other. More than a simple reach away. It's like magnets. When they get really close, you can hardly keep them apart, but if you keep them just a little further separated the strong pull can be avoided.

"You really *want* to continue to have the braces?" I had to ask again. "Even if you don't really need to?"

"I guess I do," he said. "Though you can sort of think of it as just a different means to the same ends. No matter what, I'm still stuck with something orthodontic, right? If not these, then retainers. So why not these?"

"Well...."

He laughed. "I told you these are easier. More reliable, you could say. And they definitely help with the girls."

"But you could find girls once the braces are off. You meet enough new ones, who won't have known you had them...."

"Maybe," he shrugged. "But you know what? Girls are kinds of a mystery to me. Honestly. Totally. Sometimes I think I understand them, but I don't. Braces I get. Girls I don't. But when I rely on my braces, on my understanding of what it means to have braces – that's one thing girls and I can relate to the same. Obviously only some girls, but it's a pretty big pool. So I really do think I do better with the girls with these on than I would without. Maybe it's different for you, with boys...."

I shook my head. "No. Definitely also a mystery. Baffling and frustrating."

He smiled. "The other thing is, I know who I am with braces. I don't always like it, being the guy who is pitied because he has these things and looks like that. But I know what to expect, how people will react – and I know how I can make some of them react, like the girls I open up to about it.

"If I didn't have the braces...it's kind of scary. I'd have to figure out who I was all over, and I don't think it would be that easy. Was it for you, when they came off?"

I had to think for a minute, but he was right. "No. Everyone always says how great it is to get them off. Like you're supposed to suddenly be free. But you're right, it wasn't like that. It was kind of disappointing, actually. I mean I liked how I looked, and my straight rows of teeth are great. But it didn't change my life the way everybody seemed to suggest it would."

Charles nodded.

"So how many girls with retainers have you kissed?" I asked.

"Retainers? Strictly speaking, you're the first," he laughed. "Removable appliances complicate things. Girls who get retainers want to believe they don't belong in that braced category anymore. They can remove them after all, right? So I never actually kissed a girl just with retainers like yours. It's just the ones with like sorts of functional appliances, the ones who get something like that not as a final appliance, but as part of their active treatment, that I have successfully approached."

"How about headgear?" I asked.

"None," he said. "And I think the logistics would be...too complicated. Besides, no girl ever shows herself with headgear if she doesn't have to. Other than at the orthodontist's, I never really see one. I mean other than the occasional fifth or sixth grader who has to wear it to school. But I mean, those really are just still kids.

"The funny thing is, headgear is the one guaranteed line to get a girl to fold. If they have it. You talk to them, and you sympathize, and eventually you come out with the line, *Well at least you don't have to wear headgear*, and if they do, or if they know they're going to have to, then they crumble. Because headgear is always the worst, most embarrassing secret. The final indignity."

"So do you tell them you have headgear?"

"God no!" Charles said very emphatically. "I can't hide the braces from them, and I can use them to my advantage. But headgear – that's something no one can see past. The ultimate barrier. That's why it's so devastating to them too."

"But you're not hiding yours from me."

He looked at me – that deep, deep gaze! – for what seemed like an eternity before answering. "I'm going all in. Not hiding anything. Even the ultimate thing. This thing."

My heart pounded faster at his words. It was almost scarier than someone telling me they loved me. Because it was like a complete proof of…was it love? Something like that. Something like completely giving yourself to someone else. Something I had never come close to.

I had to change the subject again, or at least back it away from this close focus on just him and me. "So you make out with all these girls?" I asked. "You eye one with braces, or some kind of orthodontia, and then you do your little sympathy dance and they fall into your arms."

He smiled and shook his head sheepishly. "It's not like that! I mean, sometimes. Surprisingly often, it works. But it's not just that, and not just about that. Some of them just want to talk. They need someone to talk to, because no one ever talks to them like that. Acknowledging their insecurities. Our insecurities. You remember that feeling when you had braces, right?"

I usually tried not to, but of course he was right. I nodded.

"Some of them just want to cry," Charles said. "And if that's all they want –someone to put their arm around them in support – I can do that too. It's not like I force myself on them. It's whatever they need. A lot of them do need or want that affirmation that some physical intimacy can give them, which they can't get that anywhere else. And a lot of them just need to cry, because having braces is so overwhelming."

"So the first girl that started blubbering…that didn't scare you off?"

Charles shook his head. "No. I expected tears to be part of it. Having braces is so emotional. And it's kind of nice just to feel needed too. To provide support like that. To be the proverbial shoulder for someone to cry on."

11.

The moms came back. You could see how they both glanced us over when they came in. Wondering what we had been up to. They couldn't hide that suspicion in their eyes. Parents are worriers, but it was funny seeing how they wondered, just for a second, just how much they had to be worried about with Charles and me. Charles's headgear helped. There was no way anyone could think anything could have happened when he had that.

And we weren't sitting completely side by side. There was that space between us on the couch. It looked all harmless and totally innocent. They couldn't begin to imagine….

"How was it?" Charles asked, and the moms gave us the highlights.

"Where are you going tomorrow?" Charles followed up.

"A couple of small town buildings," his mom said. "Some landscapes. Why? Do you want to come along?"

"Maybe," Charles said – sounding like he meant it. I tried no to look too shocked or disappointed. "If it's a nice day. Better than sitting around all day playing video games...."

"Maybe," his mother agreed.

"What time is our flight tomorrow?" he asked.

"Evening. If we leave here by six...."

Charles nodded, like he was taking it all in but pretty indifferent. He was the first to head off to bed then, saying *Good night* all around – and then winking at me.

I liked the special attention – but I had no idea what he meant.

"What about you?" Mom asked. "Do you want to join us tomorrow?"

"Maybe," I shrugged. Did I want to go if Charles went? But sitting beside him in the car for hours, unable to do anything – wouldn't it be torture? No, there was no way I was going.

Brushing my teeth and getting ready for bed, I found myself as confused as ever. Like I was unsure about what had happened during this long, strange day. And what Charles was playing at. Had he been teasing all along, with the escape hatch of going along with the moms tomorrow, leaving me high and dry?

I put my retainers in. The previous night had definitely been an exception. If I was being honest with myself, I wanted to wear them. Regardless of what Charles said. Though admittedly everything that Charles said made it easier for me to be honest with myself.

In the dark a part of me hoped Charles would sneak into my room. I knew it wouldn't happen. The way the rooms are in the guest bungalow he couldn't sneak out without his mother noticing. Much less sneak in here without my mom noticing....

Yet part of me still wished it, and imagined the possibilities....

It kept me awake, and kept me thinking. About Charles, and his crazy story. I started wondering whether he was telling the truth. Would anyone voluntarily wear their braces longer than they had to? Would any orthodontist go along with that? Wasn't it much more likely that he just really needed them longer? That he was just spinning an outlandish story for me to explain why a boy about to start eleventh grade was still stuck wearing braces? Even if the story was crazier than the much more likely reality?

But I had to admit that, even as I had been in an unbearable rush to get my braces off and couldn't wait for the day – in retrospect, I wouldn't have minded having them longer. I probably would have liked having them longer. I would have moaned and complained, but secretly I would have been happier. I'm pretty sure of that. And with what I knew from afterwards – that getting them off didn't instantly transform me into a popular princess, but left me more or less the same person I had been before – I definitely could have used another year or two of hiding behind them.

And what about his claims of seduction? Did he really do that? Did he really have any success approaching girls like that? His smooth lines worked on me – but on other girls? I guess maybe having braces was as hard for them as it had been for me. Not hard at all, in some ways – at least that's what you tried to convince your parents and the world and yourself of. And, of course, at the same time it was the most devastating, humiliating thing you could possibly imagine going through.

I could see how a sympathetic ear would be something you would turn to. Appreciate. Fall for. Yes, I might have. But still…he had braces. And they had braces.

For me it had been unimaginable kissing anyone while I had braces. That anyone would want to. Or rather it had been purely imaginable. Something that was possible in only my wildest, most far out fantasies.

Of course I never thought anyone would kiss me while I was wearing my retainers, either….

And what a kiss that had been. Actually, it had been a kiss – while everything before it, those other boys and those awkward occasions, those hadn't. They had just been fumbling liplocking by comparison. Practically just meaningless experimentation. A baby step beyond practicing kissing in the mirror or with my pillow. Kissing Charles – that had been real. What you dreamed of. What you saw in the movies.

Even though he had braces.

Sunday

1.

I blushed when I saw Charles in the morning at breakfast. To think I had wanted him to appear in my room during the night….

Of course I would have liked that. And feared that. But it had just been a daydream fantasy. An unrealistic fantasy. It was too much to hope for. Too much to expect. It was probably better – much better – than it hadn't been possible.

If he was going to join his mom on her scouting expedition after breakfast…I'd feel disappointed, but at least I'd still have my memories and fantasies. It was enough to build on. Enough to keep me smiling happily. After all, a part of me had woken up, alone in my bed, relieved. For all my raging hormones the day before, I wasn't sure if I was ready for those greater satisfactions yet.

A small part of me wanted him to go with the moms. Removing any possibility of anything more happening. The rest of me, the much larger rest prayed that maybe….

I watched him carefully, trying not to stare not too obviously. Not because of him, but because of Mom, and his mom. I didn't want to show them I cared – about him, about him spending the day with me, about anything.

Finally Mrs.Devere asked him. "Well, Charles. Do you want to come with us today?"

I prayed he wouldn't look at me before responding. I didn't want to appear too eager. I didn't want to plead, if only with my eyes. I wanted him to decide for himself. Even though I dreaded the possibility of rejection. Of him choosing the grownups and driving through the countryside over being with me.

He spooned some more of his cereal before answering. Like he still needed to weigh the options. Like it was a toss-up. Finally, he said, "Nah, I think I'll hang out here."

I tried not to sigh out loud in relief.

He turned to me. "If that's OK with you. I'm not infringing too much on your space and time, am I?"

I shrugged my best teen girl shrug. Like *Of course it's a pain, but I'll put up with it.* I could even see Mom try not to smile at my reaction. "No, it's OK."

"If you go out don't forget to lock up after you," Mom reminded me. "And just make sure to be back before five. April and Charles have to get to the airport."

"Yeah," I nodded. "Maybe we'll go to the mall. I'll see what my friends are doing. Or we can just chill here." *Chill.* My God. And even I could hear my voice quivering, trying too hard to keep cool. But Mom probably figured it was just teen girl nervousness in front of a boy. Even a boy with braces.

Charles was still sitting calmly, finishing his breakfast by the time the moms had gathered all their gear together and headed out. "So, the mall?" he asked me, smiling. He had picked up the quivering in my voice.

"Maybe not," I said, trying and managing to sound a bit more confident. Not that I felt it. My heart was certainly pounding.

"And friends you want to have over?"

"Maybe not," I repeated more firmly. Definitely not. Honestly, the embarrassment of explaining having a boy with braces staying with us to them was more trouble than anything was worth.

He nodded. Approvingly, I hoped.

"So," he said.

"So," I said.

And there we were.

He finished his milk and cleaned up. "I should go brush my teeth,' he said when he was done. I nodded. My best *Whatever* nod.

Boy, was my heart pounding.

I took a breath. But I knew what I wanted. And what I wanted to do. Which also meant I knew what I had to do. I went to my room and got my retainers out and snapped them in.

I went to the bathroom and looked at my reflection. On the one hand, I felt I looked silly. Younger. Weaker? But there was also something pleasing and reassuring about this look and feel.

It took me a few moments to gather myself. I was scared of the steps I was about to take. Scared and excited. Ready and not.

One more look, one more breath, and I went outside again.

2.

Charles was sitting on the deck with his iPad when I came out. I broke out into a smile. I couldn't help it. A nervous smile, but one you can't repress.

"You're wearing your retainers," he noticed.

"I am."

"You don't mind wearing them?"

"I want to," I said. I meant it.

Charles stood up and looked me in the eyes. That melt my heart and buckle my knees look of his. But I stared right back.

"You're sure? You thought everything over?"

I nodded.

I was prepared to talk. I didn't know exactly what I wanted to say, but I was prepared to convince him. I was sure, and I was confident I could convince him I was sure.

I wasn't prepared for him to just walk up to me and take my hand and start walking inside again. But, relieved, I let it happen. Trying not to squeeze his hand too tightly in my excitement. Hoping my palm wouldn't get all sweaty.

"Your room?" he asked.

I just nodded. I couldn't wipe the smile off my face. This was faster and more sudden than I expected – but I didn't really know what to expect.

Slowly we walked to my room, hand in hand.

We stopped in the middle. Charles turned to face me, and took my other hand. Then he leaned forward and kissed me, ever so lightly. And then he let go of my hands and pulled me closer and kissed me harder, deeper, sweeter.

When he finally pulled his face back again he looked me in the eyes and swept one hand across my hair. "You're ready for this?"

My nod was just like a fast little wobble of my head. I was bursting with readiness – and nervousness.

Charles reached for my shirt and gently pulled it over my head. I raised my arms like in surrender so he could. I almost wanted to keep them up – remembering how my breasts looked perkier that way....

He brushed my bra with the back of his hand, admiring my breasts. I began to reach behind my back to unhook it, but he smiled and put his hand on my arm. "Don't rush," he said. "Let's enjoy every moment. I got it."

He cupped my breasts, still in their bra cups, and continued to look at them, like he was imagining what was behind the fabric. I could see the bulge in his pants now – and could feel the hot moistness between my legs, as my arousal began to sweep over me.

Finally, he reached behind my back and easily unhooked the bra, kissing me as he did.. He let the straps dangle for a moment before lifting the cups, and I slipped the bra off.

Not taking his eyes off my chest, he drew in a sharp breath when my breasts were revealed. It was almost a gasp. Gently he reached for them and cupped them, brushing over one hard nipple with his thumb. He looked up at me and slowly said, "They're beautiful."

Already flushed, I blushed with pleasure. No one had ever seen my breasts. Other than my parents and doctors and things like that. No boy. Maybe glimpsed, partially, but not really seen. Not *admired*, the way Charles was doing.

He kneaded them gently, he lightly squeezed and brushed against the nipples that were now so hard they almost hurt. He bent over and put one in his mouth, and I could feel the flicks of his tongue, and the metallic roughness of the braces that he carefully pressed against them. I couldn't stifle a moan, and then another.

I wanted to rip my pants off but I waited. I let Charles lead me along. Even as I trembled from the excitement and the satisfaction. This was already more and better than what I had imagined possible. I already felt more than I ever had.

Charles kissed me again, one hand on a breast the other on my bare back. And then his hand moved down to my pants and unbuttoned them and then lowered the zipper. I tried to keep myself from moaning as I felt this hand down there. Even through the double layer of clothes, I was so sensitive now that it set off sensations that took me much longer to achieve by myself.

My pants open, he began to pull them loose around my hips, and then I helped and pulled them down and off. Leaving me standing there in my underwear. Not the most embarrassing pair I had, I was relieved to realize.

Instead of pulling my panties off too he began unbuttoning his own shirt, and then let me take over. Taking it off revealed his buff body – not ridiculously rippling just with muscles, but toned and firm.

He opened and pulled off his pants, and then pulled down his underpants, leaving him standing there naked close in front of me. His erect penis pointed up at me at a steep angle. I tried not to show any surprise, but I hadn't really ever seen one of these things up close and personal. In the flesh. And it was so much flesh.

He took my hands and cupped them underneath his hairy scrotum. I could feel the two oddly shaped testicles in them.

I kneeled down in front of him, to get a better look and feel.

I ran one hand over the massive, erect tool. The skin was so smooth, almost silky. Delicate. Until the almost heart-shaped pale-purple tip, a rawer flesh looking more like my gums than skin.

A bead – a tear – glistened on the tip of his penis. My tongue darted out before I could even begin to think about it. The salty sweet taste exploded in my mouth.

I couldn't keep myself from taking the whole cock in my mouth – frustrated now by my retainers that seemed to inhibit how much of it I could grasp and feel orally.

But I just drew it in and sucked it in deep only once before slowly releasing it again, now covered in a film of moisture. I marveled at how hard it was – not completely ungiving, but the skin taut over what felt like a piece of pure muscle.

I had seen penises on YouTube and TV, but his seemed wider and larger than most of those I had seen. Not enormous, but bigger than I expected. With friends I had played around imagining what it was like, and we read that six inches length was normal – but his was surely at least eight. And maybe it wasn't two inches wide, but certainly an inch and half....

"Is that bigger than usual?" I had to ask him.

He smiled. "I've never compared it in…this state. But maybe it's on the larger size than you should usually expect."

My heart pounded more strongly. Maybe a slimmer, more boyish one would have made for an easier initiation? Was I ready for his man-sized tool? But even if it hurt…I *wanted* it.

He hooked his thumb into the elastic of my panties and tugged, but in my eagerness I rushed ahead of him, swiftly pulling them down and off.

His palm and fingers pressed against my hairy triangle, and he turned me so that he stood behind me. Considerably taller, his erect cock now pressed in the small of my back against my spine like a rod to hold it straight, his balls dangling on top of my ass. His right hand clutched my sopping cunt, the other wrapped around and held a breast, and he leaned down to kiss my neck.

It was all I could do to keep from moaning at all the pleasures I felt on so many sides of my body With my eyes closed I could almost imagine three or four of him pleasuring me – and I shuddered at the realization that all his touches were still simply on the surface....

Releasing me – before I collapsed into a shuddering, ecstatic mess on the floor – he took my hand and pulled me over to the bed. My heart fluttered with increased nervousness, knowing I was being led to getting fucked. Fucked for the first time.

I lay down. Leaning on my side, head propped on my elbow. Trying to look sexy or seductive. He smiled at my efforts, but gently pushed me to lie down on my back. He moved to the bottom of the bed, and then up towards me. I had to spread my legs to accommodate him, leaving me feeling more vulnerable and exposed.

Already spread-eagled, he pushed my legs even farther apart as he knelt between them, staring down at my bushy cunt. Did he mind that I didn't shave or wax it? Girls talked about that, but I had never dared. I think Mom would have been pretty shocked if I did.

He bent over and put his face to my crotch. I felt his nose rub against the lips of my labia and then heard him sniff and inhale. If the tremors of pleasure hadn't overwhelmed me I would have worried about the smell – would he like it? should I have cleaned myself better? – but before I could even try to gather those thoughts I felt the soft rounded tip of his tongue dart at my clitoris and then more of his tongue dip into my cunt, it's slightly rough surface rubbing me in all the right ways.

He continued to penetrate me lightly like this – more than licking, but the gentle, giving softness of his tongue against clit and labias enough to bring me to states of arousal that I had barely ever reached with my own manual manipulations.

I squirmed, unable to keep still as the surge of pleasure radiating from my clit expanded through me, I couldn't stifle my moans – and just as I thought I couldn't bear it any longer he pulled his face away. I thought I had a moment to catch my breath but before I even knew it he had slid his body up – and plunged his cock into me, in one smooth, powerful, almost endlessly extended motion. It seemed to keep coming, this fleshy rod that he slid and slid deeper into me, forcing my legs even wider apart as his hips thrust up against mine.

I almost fainted overwhelmed. It was so *much* – and would have been unbearable but for the pleasure that came with it as he slid into me, an orgasmic release of such incredible potency. I had no more control over anything, crying, laughing, and groaning with the unending ecstasy I was feeling, my tongue running over the smooth surfaces of my retainers while I gasped for breath.

And then he started thrusting in and out, slowly at first and then with increasing rapidity and I was helpless, hopeless, barely able to handle all the sensations I was feeling. He was tearing me apart yet holding me together, there was pain but it only enhanced my pleasure – and my pleasure was beyond anything I could have ever even imagined. I came and came and came, until finally I could feel him slow for some final, more deliberate thrusts, and then I could feel the burst of ejaculate shooting out and we both came together one final, spectacular time.

I could feel his penis soften slightly as he completed a few more final thrusts, the overwhelming tool finally not pressing as hard all around inside me, and then he finally withdrew and slid off me, lying down beside me.

I was still gasping for air, still drenched in sweat – and a headier mix of juices down below – but I welcomed his kisses as he leaned his head over mine. His tongue against my retainers, mine against his braces – how beautiful the feel of the rough metal of those braces!

I was crying and smiling. What an experience! My friends passed on stories about sexual experiences – hardly any first-hand, so probably even more skewed and twisted than the truth – and there were those concerns about how it can hurt, or how quickly boys are satisfied, before we could be. Like every teen boy had to be a premature ejaculator!

But this had been almost nothing like I expected. The pain hadn't been the hurt I expected – no hymen-tearing roughness, it was only the sheer size of his cock that was almost too much. Even as it was ultimately perfect – this had been that good sort of pain that you want to prolong and feel more of. And far from coming too fast, Charles seemed to have incredible stamina – I was the one who kept thinking, *this has to be it, this has to be the highpoint, it can't go on*, only for Charles to take it up another notch.

I had been as curious about sex as everyone, but I had expected it to be a mixture of the awkward, uncomfortable, and pleasurable. I could never have imagined it to be this good. Out of nothingness – nothingness and *braces* – Charles had conjured up an entirely new world of experience for me.

3.

Even minutes later I was still breathing hard. Like after the most exhausting athletic competition. Not a marathon, but a long, extended sprint.

I couldn't wipe the smile off my face either. And I could still feel the tingle of pleasure aching in the depths of my cunt.

And though I couldn't believe I was wearing them, I appreciated the bulk of my retainers in my mouth.

Lying on my side, Charles on his, facing me, we smiled at each other and continued to exchange kisses. We still hadn't said a word, basking only in the afterglow of our complete physical union.

I looked at grinning Charles – into his eyes, but also at his braces. A sight I had never expected to see when I first turned to a man after making love to him. They looked ridiculous on him, of course – they were braces – but perfect too. I kept wanting to kiss him, to feel them, and kept thinking how much more perfect to have them there than if all there was was the white flatness of unbraced teeth.

"So was that alright?" he finally asked, smiling. He knew it had been alright.

"It was," I said. "It was perfect."

He reached forward with his index finger and lightly touched the wire of my retainer. "Even with those?"

"These and those," I said, touching his braces with the tip of my index finger.

Would it have been better if we had both been orthodontia-free? For the movie version, maybe. But without our orthodontia it would never even have happened, would it? We would never even gotten this far. Not close. And found the same, necessary connection. And what surprised me more, the additional features – the feel of the bulk of acrylic in my mouth, the metal in his – enhanced rather than encumbered the act itself. They made it even more physical and sensual. If the sex alone would have rated 99 out of a 100 anyway, the braces and my retainers were the final touch that put it over the top to perfection.

"So what was it like for you to have braces?" Charles asked, finally breaking a long silence.

I was not really surprised he brought up the subject. It was hardly out of the blue. It was front and center, here – and always, I began to realize.

It's not what anyone would think of as a post-coital talking point – but really, what could have been more intimate? I had revealed everything to him. I was now even lying there in the nude in front of him. Among the few things left still hidden from him, the important things about me, was that. Though in some ways I think he knew even better than I did what it had meant to me. He seemed to understand everything about this – about having braces, about having sex – better than I did. Like his insistence on my wearing the retainers: I know he said it was for his sake, but with the reassuring comfort of them in my mouth I realized how important it had been for me, too.

My time in braces was something I hadn't really ever talked about with anyone. I had *had* braces, but I had never really talked about all that meant, at the time or afterwards. My parents, my friends...at the time, they mouthed the obligatory words and pretended or wished it wasn't a big deal. Afterwards, no one ever wanted to bring it up. No one dared say everything there really was to say.

And, in opening up, I really understood how Charles could connect with girls who were dealing with that. Who wanted to unburden themselves, or at least share their feelings about that enormous burden. Because no one else was willing to, and there he was patient, caring – and braced.

I think he knew I wanted to talk about my braces.

And it was embarrassing sharing a lot of that. It sounded so silly. They were just braces, for heaven's sake. But he understood. That was what was so wonderful. He really understood.

I was emotional from the sex too, of course, but the tears that came were also because of the release of finally being able to open up about what I had repressed so long. How hard it had been to have braces – especially since everyone tried to pretend it was something that shouldn't be hard at all, and the misguided sympathy was for the stuff that hardly mattered, like the pain after they got tightened.

Charles understood, and he listened, and he stroked me and kissed me when I needed it. And it was such an incredible relief to just babble – lisping thickly with my retainers – about stuff that everyone else would have dismissed as insignificant and over with.

I only got to one of the most important things last, something I'd barely really admitted to myself and certainly not said out loud.

I began by confessing, "When you said about the orthodontist strapping your wrists down...I was kind of jealous. I could have so used that! Like every time. I *never* know what to do with my hands at the orthodontist – and to have them restrained is like ideal!"

Charles nodded. "It is."

"When I got my braces," I worked up my nerve to tell him, "well, my orthodontist is part of a big practice. There are a couple of orthodontists, and lots of examination rooms. And the layout of the practice is pretty open. When you walk down the wide halls you can see into the large examination rooms, which usually have more than one examination chair. There's a lot of activity. Coming and going. And I mean when you're in the chair you almost don't notice, because of...well, what's happening to you. But people walk by, and often there's someone else being treated at the same time in a chair nearby.

"So the first two times my mom takes me, for all the stuff they have to do to see what kind of braces you need, and to prepare what's necessary for them, I probably sit in three different examination chairs in three different rooms. It's a bit dizzying, because you also go for X-rays and photographs in other rooms, but the staff take charge and you just follow and it's fine. Of course I was kind of nervous, and hardly thrilled about what this was leading up to, but it's like at any medical professional's. They sort of drag you through it – because for them you're mostly just a number, and probably already the seventeenth that day, and so they can't treat it totally like it is for you. For you it's a once in a lifetime experience."

"Usually," Charles reminded me, flashing his braces.

"Right. And that's OK, though. Maybe even easier than if they try to be too chummy, because that comes across as dishonest. I could tell that I was just another kid for my orthodontist, but she was still very friendly and professional, and so that was OK for the most part.

"She keeps me informed about what she's doing, and what the next steps are, too. And there's the conversation with her and Mom, where she tells us more or less what my treatment is going to involve, and how long it is going to take, and Mom nods of course and agrees and says *OK*. Meaning we are going ahead with it, and we all understand that that means that at the next appointment. I am getting braces.

"So there's no big surprise in store. The orthodontist explained what they'd look like, and even if you can never imagine it until you have them, at least I had as good a sense as one can have. And I sort of knew what the procedure would involve. Even though you can never truly understand what it's like until you go through it, you sort of have an idea.

"I count down the days, and nights, and then the day comes, and Mom drives me to the orthodontist and after a wait that seems like forever even though it's just like ten minutes an assistant comes out to ask whether I'm ready to get my braces. Which is an awful question, but that's what I'm there for, so I nod.

"Mom doesn't come into the examination room with me. She tries to play it cool, but I can tell that she can't bear to watch. She asks me if I want her to be there for support, but I'm in sixth grade, I'm old enough, I can handle this. Besides, I can see that she wouldn't be great support....

"She hugs me, and then she gives me one of those looks like I'm going in for life-threatening surgery and she might never see me again – and it's true that she sort of won't see me again, not like this. I'll have braces. And of course I don't understand yet what it means to go from not having them to having them, but Mom does, and that's why she's looking at me so sadly and wishes she could do anything to make this easier, but knows she can't.

"I only process all that in the back of my mind. I already have my own nerves and fears to deal with. Which aren't the unusual tangible terror, but that great, vague fear of the complete unknown. Even though I know what's coming – braces! – deep down I also have this sense that I don't understand the magnitude of it yet. Which of course turns out to be true.

"I follow the assistant, and I'm sort of relieved we don't go into one of the first examination rooms, where more people pass by and which seem to be busier. And also just to put off this happening even just for a few more seconds....

"But we keep walking. And keep walking. All the way to the end of the hall. Farther than I've ever gone before. And we come to a room with a door. Even the orthodontist's office doesn't have a door, so this is unusual.

"The assistant opens the door into a pretty large examination room, but there's only one chair, like a throne in the middle of it, and there seem to be a few more elaborate gadgets around. And dangling from the chair I notice there are quite a few straps.

"Closing the door behind her, the assistant has me sit down in the chair, and she takes the first strap, which is like a seat belt, and fastens it around my waist. And she explains that she's going to buckle me. 'Sort of like your car seat, when you were young," she explains. Only then does she ask, 'OK?'

"Of course, she isn't asking, she's saying, and even as she's talking she pulls up a strap between my legs and buckles that into the seat belt, and then fastens belts that come down over my shoulders, and one across my chest. So I can't slide around in the chair.

"Later someone mentions that sometimes they still have patients who they put to sleep for the installation procedure, and this way they can't slip down in the seat, but the orthodontist seems to like it this way even when the patient is awake.

"I'm really surprised, and a bit embarrassed at being tied down like this. But what I barely dare admit to myself is how relieved I am. It's comfortable, for one thing, being held in place like that. And it's almost like a weight off my shoulders. I know I have to submit to this procedure – and being strapped down helplessly makes it so much easier.

"But I can't believe they didn't strap my hands down! That's the one thing that was missing. That would have made it even better."

Charles laughed. "Now I'm jealous of you! My orthodontist only used the wrist restraints, but this sounds so much better!"

"Not without the wrist restraints," I insisted.

"So the procedure then, that was OK?"

"It was...I was so relaxed. She put in that cheek retractor, and everything was fine. And it was only when she was done that everything began to sink in. And then she brought my mom in, before she took the cheek retractor out. And...well, it was exactly like you said with yours. She really tried to hide her shock and disappointment, but you could just see it in her eyes and expression, how devastated she was. And of course when I got my first look, when the orthodontist handed me the mirror, I fell apart. Because...well, I had braces."

"Did you get to get your follow-up appointments in that chair too?"

"No. I wish I had had the nerve to request it, like you did. I always prayed they'd take me there, but I never dared ask them to put me there. It only happened two more times, I guess when the other chairs were filled.

"One of those times, going there, I passed a girl from school coming out. And we both looked at each other, knowing she had just been strapped down and I was just about to be, and it was like a shared pleasure and embarrassment. But neither of us ever, ever said anything to each other about it. Even Mom never asked about the chair, or mentioned it."

"Orthodontists should definitely encourage their patients to make their feelings known better," Charles said.

"I think my feelings were buried under so much embarrassment and shame that I wouldn't have been able to admit to a tenth of it. I mean, I've never been able to talk about almost any of this until now – until I'm naked, with a boy. A boy who has braces...."

Charles nodded like he'd heard that more than once before.

4.

Charles got us two waters from the kitchen. I was so thirsty that I downed mine almost in a single swallow.

Pleasantly exhausted I lay down on my stomach, my head resting on my crossed arms, looking at Charles sitting on the side of the bed, sipping more slowly at his water.

His penis dangled between his legs, not shriveled but drooping, curved instead of tautly erect – but still showing some signs of life.

Putting down the water, he looked me over again, smiling. I think he liked what he saw. He reached out and put one had on my curved butt, rubbing it lightly. From the rise it got out of him, between his legs, I could be sure he liked *that*.

"Boys are going to like that," he said. "Men," he said, giving a playful squeeze to my ass, and then letting his hand slide down between my cheeks until his middle finger came down all the way between my labia. I liked *that*.

"In fact, that's probably something you should be prepared for," he said. "A lot of boys seem to like this side too. We probably should have a stab at that as well," he side, getting up.

I wasn't sure what he meant and propped myself up on my elbows.

He went to the bathroom, and came back with a tube of some lotion. Then he picked up his pants and got something out of his wallet. A condom, I realized when he sat down beside me.

His cock was already firm, and pointing up again as he sat down on the edge of the bed again. He opened the condom wrapper and pulled it out. "Lubricated," he emphasized, holding the glistening, rolled up latex sheath briefly before pulling it down over his penis. Pretty much like the demonstration in health class. Except the banana was way more curved than his cock.

I smiled and began to turn, to lie on my back and spread my legs again, but he pulled me back, "No, no," he said, pulling me so I turned and was lying on my stomach.

He opened the tube he had brought from the bathroom. "Not actual lubricant, but it should help smooth passage a bit at least," he said.

Before I could react, he wiped a big dollop of cream, between my butt cheeks, and I could feel the cold ooze uncomfortably near my sphincter.

"Wait," I tried to protest, but he was still holding me down with the one hand and before I could adjust he was sitting on the back of my thighs straddling me.

"Wait," I repeated. "I don't really think I'm up for that...." I wasn't even sure about his intentions – he couldn't want to do *that*, could he?

Leaning over me – pinning me down even more securely, though in a perfectly natural, not intimidating way, just a consequence of how I lay under him – he spoke into my ear. "I know it's a bit scary, but men are going to want this from you. Better to have experienced it once, to be able to say whether or not you're willing to do it."

But I didn't feel very willing – not if he was thinking of doing what it seemed like he was thinking of doing. Even the thought of being penetrated in my rear.... My girlfriends and I joked about it sometimes. None of us said we could imagine it – though some looked as if they were at least curious. Of course it was that way with talking about taking a boy's cock in our mouths too. Some thought that was totally disgusting, but when faced with the real thing I could barely keep myself from lunging to it. But this was something different. Even if it didn't sound like it was as...sensory. With in-your-face oral sex you had taste and smell to deal with, beyond just the feel. With this, there wasn't that. Instead... I still couldn't even imagine it. Having something that big shoved in there.

Even the words for it were so ugly. *Anal sex. Sodomy.* I didn't want to do that.

I felt Charles other hand begin to rub the cream. Not with his finger but a knuckle. Massaging, probing where my ass was clenched tightly closed. "Relax," he murmured.

I tried to buckle, but he was so much stronger and heavier than me. I could barely move. More desperately, I said, "Charles, really, I don't think I want to do this."

"I know it's scary," he repeated softly. "Just relax." And he continued massaging.

I squirmed under him. Not desperately, but in frustration. This wasn't a situation or position I had ever imagined myself in. "Charles, please, don't," I said.

"Just let yourself go," he said, his voice still so gentle but insistent. "Relax. Relax."

I clenched my buttocks as tight as I could. Not even on purpose – it was the natural reaction. Didn't that already send enough of a message? No entry.

He didn't force anything. He didn't push hard. But he kept slowly moving and probing. I couldn't hold out, and I felt the knuckle enter, ever so slightly, the forbidden zones that nothing had ever penetrated.

"There's a good girl," Charles said.

I didn't struggle. Maybe I should have? But I was impotent against his weight and strength, wasn't I? "Please, Charles," I said, "I don't think I'm ready...." Would he listen to that?

"Relax," he said, and I felt the lubricated knuckle widen the path. Half an inch, an inch.

"There we go," he said, and now I could feel his fingers, placeholders at the edge of my abyss. I still didn't think I wanted to go there.

My protest was feeble when I felt him shift his body, pushing my legs further apart and lowering himself slowly on me. And then I felt the maneuver as he slipped his fingers out and they were replace by the round head of his cock, which he managed to get just that first inch in preventing me from clenching my ass closed again.

"Relax," he said, gently.

I couldn't help but begin to cry at my impotence. At not wanting this to happen – and at that lingering question challenging me from within, that sharp doubt, that small part of me that was excited about this happening. Something I was fighting almost harder than the assault itself.

Was this what it was like to be raped? It felt like a sort of violation. It was against my will – even as my will struggled against itself. No small part of me was relieved I was being forced into it – because I could never desire or ask this to be done to be. (*Like getting braces!* I couldn't help but think....) I wanted to refuse to admit that part of me wanted it. But in my powerlessness – hadn't the choice been taken from me? – it also felt like a violation. Maybe like a sort of date rape, where you go along with it because you can't extricate yourself from it after having gone so far....

"Relax," Charles said, and slowly but surely continued to forge ahead, and I could feel his huge cock penetrating, oh so slowly, deeper.

(I did know how I could stop him. Just take out my retainer. He might be deaf to my words or cries, or know they couldn't be fully trusted, but he would understand that. Instantly.

I didn't take out my retainers)

Sobbing, I finally gave up all resistance – which instantly made it easier and lessened the discomfort, but also allowed him to glide more gently deeper and deeper in. I couldn't believe how far his tool went as it kept slowly, slowly progressing, and then going still farther. I couldn't believe there was room there. I couldn't believe it found a place. There. I truly felt like I was impaled on his cock.

Finally, after what seemed an eternity, and after what seemed to fill me far beyond any possible physical tolerance, I could feel his hips against by ass. He was literally entirely inside me. I gasped, barely able to take a breath.

Gently he began to pull back, but only partway, then pushed back in, establishing the rhythm of sex in a slow motion. It was thoughtful, meant to cause me as little pain as possible, but the strange feeling of his cock up my ass was still a lot to take in. But as I stopped resisting, as I let him have his way, the warmth of an unexpected arousal began to spread across me too.

It wasn't like the vaginal sex had been, yet it offered its own sensual pleasures – much to my surprise. And almost to my disappointment – what little rational part was left to me didn't *want* to derive enjoyment from being ass-fucked. But the sensual part of me that had taken almost completely over lapped up these newfound, almost unbearably heightened feelings.

Once he established a slow, slow rhythm I could feel Charles's hand reach under my belly and slide down towards my cunt, and he began to let his fingers dance and play there, heightening my arousal. Crying still I found myself being taken to new peaks of arousal out of nowhere by his stimulation, and before I even knew it I had already come – hearing Charles wince as my orgasmic tensing squeezed him in his steady in and half-out motions. But he persevered. He didn't even change the slow rhythm he'd established, and with each push in I felt on the verge of coming again – until I did with a throaty cry and shiver, all resistance and will collapsing in me.

Only when he was close to coming did the thrusts become more vigorous and longer again, and I could feel him ready himself for his own explosion, and with that final plunge and the short jerks to finish him off I came like a smaller aftershock along with him.

I was literally gasping as I felt him slowly pull his cock out. He pulled his hand away from my cunt and I could feel him reach between my ass, to hold the condom on his cock as he withdrew it.

He pulled out, and my tender, battered, tired sphincter closed the opening off again.

I could barely move, and I didn't. I lay there, gasping for air, almost delirious from the sensations – explosions that were beyond any pleasure I had previously thought possible, along with a deep soreness in my ass.

I could see Charles walk to the bathroom. Hear him flush the condom, and then run some water to wash his hands.

He came down and sat on the edge of the bed again. Tears still trickled from my eyes. Of relief and humiliation and anger. I looked at him and expected him to apologize, but he just smiled, and then reached out to pull the sweaty, matted hair from my face.

After a minute of silence he leaned forward and kissed me. I barely reacted. In my exhaustion maybe I could barely react. I wanted to be angry but I wasn't angry. If anything, I was grateful – and angry with myself for feeling grateful, and so satisfied.

Charles lay down beside me again. He seemed to understand everything, even without speaking. He seemed to understand everything so well. Like you want in a guide – and he was my guide in our voyage through this strange new territory. The heat radiating off his body pulled me to it like a magnet again. We became as one without becoming as one *that* way, just skin on skin, head to toe, limbs intertwined.

His penis was still gorged with blood, but not fully erect. I couldn't keep from cradling it in my hand.

He kissed me again, and now I responded. I couldn't not.

"Do you want to take those out now?" he asked, putting the tip of his index finger to my lips and teeth.

I didn't even have to think about it. I didn't *want* to think about it. I shook my head. The retainers were my solace and salvation, a hold when he had done what he had done. What we had done. My retainers made all this possible, and even if all this was now truly overwhelming – a lifetime's experience in a few hours – they provided the small interior stability and support that kept me from crumbling under the weight of all it.

In Charles's arms, with him gently kissing me – and with the retainers firmly, fully in my mouth – I felt happier and more complete than I ever had.

5.

Time, and feeling, were a blur. A thick haze of emotions. His body aligned with mine, my curves wending, flesh on flesh, with his. As one. Face to face, I couldn't stop bringing my mouth to his, alternately softly and then deeply kissing him.

The braces, gleaming so close, now were not repellant but drew me in. The fine latticework of metal, the elastics reining them in – I was *glad* he had these. Glad I faced these. Glad I could enjoy these. He wouldn't be nearly the man or lover without them, I realized. Superficially more agreeable – but it was the braces that made him. And my mouth kept being pulled to them, and him.

"So do you have any more desires? Any wishes to fulfil?" he asked, like fairy tale prince that can make anything happen. Make anything true.

We'd covered all the orifices. He'd taken my virginity, and he'd fucked me up the ass. I'd felt the full throb of his organ in my mouth. I'd experienced more than I could have dared imagine I could do with a man. Of course I was satisfied. And of course I was still hungry.

I turned, lying on my back, staring dreamily up. Charles propped himself up on one elbow – and couldn't resist reaching for my breast, gently running his hand over it, the erect nipple brushing sensitively against it.

What did I want? What did I fantasize about? I wasn't used to *admitting* these things. Not out loud, not to anyone. They were buried secrets that I dreamt of under the cover of darkness, at night, alone in my bed….

But I had shared everything with Charles. He saw me – he was seeing me in my retainers, which almost felt like more of an exposure than my nudity. He had penetrated me, to the core of my soul and my body.

I eyed the headboard and the bedposts. I bit my lip. I dared suggest, "You could tie me to the bed…."

He looked slightly surprised but his smile suggested he wasn't shocked by the suggestion. "You want me to tie you up – and then fuck you?"

I nodded, still biting my lip. Part of me was afraid he would agree to do it. Part – including the moistening folds between my legs – wished nothing more.

"The bedposts? Limbs spread out?" he asked.

I nodded, shyly but eagerly.

He seemed to be thinking about it and then nodded. "We can do that."

He sat up. "Do you have some rope? Or something we can use?"

I blushed. I didn't want it to seem that I was actually prepared for this. But I sort of was....

I got up and went to the closet. There was a bag there. Different stuff, but some from my Halloween costume from the previous fall. I had gone goth. Which was so not me. Which was why it had been a great costume. And part of the costume had been four wide, studded leather cuffs, with rings dangling from them, like on dog collars for a leash. I had found them in a thrift store – they were perfect for the costume. And, I thought, for this.

I didn't just think, I knew. I had sort of tried it out. All by myself. Putting the cuffs on my wrists and ankles. Tying pieces of rope to the bedposts at the foot of my bed. Securing them to the loops. Then one longer piece of rope, attached to the two wrist cuffs and then lobbed over the headboard. I couldn't do it so my arms and legs were really stretched out, but it gave me a bit of a feeling for what it could be like. And I liked the feeling.

Of course I hadn't ever *really* tried it. Given up control. Let someone tie me up like this. Once or twice I had been tempted to suggest it, when I was fooling around with friends. But it would be hard not reveal how seriously I meant it, and I was way too embarrassed to admit that.

I had sort of explored something like this at a sleepover with a friend earlier that year. We had watched a movie in which someone gets tied up. Just her hands behind her back. And we were both kind of curious. We jokingly kept bringing it up, and finally dared to wonder aloud *What would it be like?* and both sort of egged each other on to try it. I think we could each tell the other was more than just curious, too, but we pretended not to take it seriously and treated it like a game.

I tied her hands behind her back first. With the flannel belt from her bathrobe. 'Properly, so I really can't get out,' she insisted. She wanted to give up control. And then I blindfolded her. I didn't really know what else to do, so I told her I was going to go watch some more TV, and I pretended to leave the room, but I just closed the door so it sounded like I had left and stood there. She hadn't protested, and she sat there quietly, but you could tell she kind of liked it.

After a couple of minutes I pretended to come back in, and I got up all in her face and asked if I should release her. She said 'Yes,' but it kind of sounded like she would have preferred me to leave her that way longer.

Then she tied my hands behind my back and it was amazing how instantly powerless I felt. And how I liked that feeling. She blindfolded me too, and she debated aloud whether to stay or go. I said she should stay, and she sat down opposite me, and she put her hands on my sides, on my ribcage, and I could feel her face close to mine, and she wondered aloud how a boy would take advantage of the situation. My heart pounded so much I was sure she could see it through my top. And I would never have said it, but I kind of hoped she would move her hands to my chest, and I even imagined her kissing me. Imagining that I could pretend it was a boy kissing me.

I think the only reason nothing happened was because she still had braces. For both of us it was unthinkable that you would kiss anyone when you had braces. Completely more unimaginable than kissing a girl. Blindfolded, I could have pretended it wasn't a girl. We both could have pretended we were just experimenting. But the braces got in the way. We couldn't imagine those away, or imagine a way around them.

Eventually she undid the blindfold. Still sitting right in front of me. And from the way she looked at me – and I'm sure from the way I looked at her – you could tell we were both sorry that she hadn't. Or she couldn't. But she had the braces....

I laid out the four cuffs on the bed.

Charles smiled. "These will do nicely," he agreed.

I found the pieces of cord I had used rolled up on a shelf in my closet too, and I tossed those on the bed.

I went to the bathroom, to pee and splash some cold water on my face. As if to wake myself up – the thought *Am I really doing this?* hitting me just as hard as the icy water.

I looked at myself in the mirror. Naked. But no longer the girl I had been when I got up in the morning. Maybe not really a woman yet, either. But much closer than a few hours ago.

I liked the body I saw in the mirror. I didn't have anything to be embarrassed about. Or not too much, anyway. My breasts could be bigger? But Charles seemed to like them....

I smiled, revealing the two wires of my retainers. My first thought was the same thought I always had, drilled into me by everyone's reaction. How silly they looked. How childish they looked. How humiliating. But I forced myself to keep my teeth bared, instead of quickly covering up the shameful sight like I always did. And I had to admit Charles was right, that there was a certain elegance to their silvery simplicity. Beauty, even.

And running my tongue over the acrylic bulk filling my mouth I enjoyed the continuing satisfaction of that feeling.

I stared one more time. Was I ready for this? Maybe not entirely, I realized, my heart pounding so hard. But I couldn't resist.

I came back out and sat down on the bed by Charles. I held out my hands.

"You sure about this?" Charles asked.

I tried not to show any doubt. More for my own sake than his. "Yes," I insisted.

He strapped one cuff tight around my wrist. Then the other. Then he got down on the floor and strapped one around each ankle. All tight and secure. I realized I wouldn't be able to slip out of them, like I probably could have when I had tried it on my own.

Sitting back on the bed beside me, he pulled my feet onto the bed and took a piece of rope and threaded it through the rings on one of the cuffs on my ankle. Knotted it tightly. Then the other.

"OK," he said, getting up. "Lie down," he told me.

I did.

He took the loose end of one of the ropes and tied it to the bottom bedpost. Close to the post itself. If I arched my foot, my toes could touch the bedpost.

He walked around to the other side of the bed and took the other loose rope, and pulled it towards him. I slid down and over further, and he pulled my foot almost to the bedpost.

My bed is really wide, so my legs were really spread far apart. But I could slide down as much as I needed, so it wasn't that awkward.

I felt a similar pang like when the orthodontist assistant buckled me into the seat as I watched Charles tie and knot the other cord. I was tied down, but I could still release myself – if I wanted to. But, like at the gynecologist's, when she made me sit in the stool with the stirrups and then spread my legs apart, I was already terribly exposed and vulnerable.

"Well?" Charles smiled.

I held out my cuffed hands. My heart pounding.

Charles took my pillows and arranged them one on top of the other for me to recline on. I lay back on them – not flat on the bed now, but my head and the upper part of my torso, supported by the pillows, up at a slight angle.

Charles took my right wrist and threaded a piece of rope through the loop. Tied it fast. And pulled the other end to the bedpost, stretching my arm out. Then tying the rope to the bedpost.

Only one hand left free. Still enough if I wanted to escape. I felt a pang of worry and of fear. And a greater shiver of excitement. I held my hand out for him as Charles moved to the other side of the bed.

He repeated the procedure, fastening the rope to the cuff, then pulling it to the bedpost. Only he pulled harder now, stretching me further, closer, before tying it fast.

Then he moved back to the other side, undid the knot and pulled that tighter too, truly stretching me in all four directions. Not painfully, but seriously limiting my mobility. I could flop my hands and arms around quite a bit – but I couldn't reach very far. I couldn't reach my mouth to remove my retainers, for example. Not that I wanted to.

"A blindfold....," Charles muttered.

"There's an eye mask in the night stand drawer," I told him.

He got it out and sat on the bed beside me. He put it on my head, but just over my forehead for now. He looked deeply into my eyes. Passionately, it seemed to me. He kissed me, gently but firmly, the metal rubbing lightly against lips.

"You're going to get fucked, you know that, right?" he said sweetly.

I couldn't suppress my smile or hide my eagerness. I tried not to twist under the bonds. I nodded.

"Blindfolded," he said, pulling the eye mask over my eyes and shutting me off from the most dominant of my senses. "So you can imagine whoever you want is having his way with you. Even someone without braces."

I could, I realized – but I didn't want to. I didn't want to imagine anyone else, just him. And I didn't want to imagine him without braces....

6.

Charles made me wait. Quivering with anticipation. I could feel him sitting on the bed, his weight causing the mattress to sag slightly towards him. But he didn't move.

Finally I felt his weight shift slightly – and a hand on my breast, as he began to ply it. Expertly. Titillatingly.... I arched my back and couldn't suppress a moan. Tied down, deprived of sight, I was even more hyperaware – and eager.

But Charles continued to be patient, allowing me only the small senses of satisfaction even as I longed for the bigger release.

Finally his hand moved to my other breast – and his mouth came down on the vacated one. A paroxysm shook me, before I sank into the delirium of him sinking his mouth onto my breast.

Still licking and teasingly nipping at my breast, his hand moved down to between my legs. Instinctively I tried to pull them slightly together – but I couldn't, I couldn't. They were bound fast, spread wide open.

For a moment I worried about the sopping wetness his fingers encountered there, but nothing in his movements suggested it bothered him at all. He played, with his palm and his fingers, in the folds of my swollen mons, teasing at the edge. Desperately I arched my back to offer it up even more obviously, but he refused to sink into my depths yet.

I was so ready to receive him, and arched my back again as he moved himself between my legs – but only to put his face in my crotch. I could feel his nose, and then his mouth as he hungrily caressed me there with lips, tongue, and the barest brushes of his braces.

Cruelly he darted his tongue into me – shallowly, briefly – before circling back and around my clitoris. I thrashed under my bonds now, desperate for release and satisfaction, my extremities bound fast even as I could move my hips to invite him.

I began to come – and just as I did he plunged into me. Deeper and deeper and as my orgasm rose up through me, my body trying to shake but barely able to under his weight now pressing onto and into me.

As I recovered he began thrusting in and out – deep, long, deliberate thrusts, like he was trying to see how far he could penetrate and then slowly withdrawing, again and again.

As I began to feel my next orgasm grip me he sped up thrusting faster and faster and harder, pounding into me and against me. I moaned uncontrollably – I'd lost all control, and would have just been thrashing wildly about if I hadn't been so tightly tied down.

Only as we came did he slow down again, and did a final purr and sigh come from my hoarse throat.

7.

We lay there. Panting. Recovering.

After a few minutes Charles pulled the eye mask off and smiled down at me. My heart practically melted at the sight – even as I was embarrassed that someone with such ridiculous braces could arouse such passionate strong feelings in me.

"Was that good?" he asked.

"It was good," I said, lifting my head slightly so that he would kiss me. He understood, and he did.

I sighed and sank back on the pillow again. Sweaty, my hands and feet tied spread all apart, my retainers filling my mouth – and yet I had never felt more elated. Never better. If I could save that moment for eternity.... I hadn't ever known such happiness. Not that I could recall.

I was glad that Charles didn't begin to release me right away. *Could I stay this way forever?* I dreamed. At least for a few minutes I could dream that, and Charles must have seen from the happiness on my face that I wanted nothing to change, not immediately.

Finally he began undoing the ropes. First my feet, then my hands. I sat up in the bed and let him take me in his arms. I hugged him tight. I began sobbing. The emotion of it all, and the physical exhaustion, overwhelmed me.

"Thank you," I whispered in his ear.

He seemed to understand – everything. And he continued to hold me tight.

Finally I wiped away my tears and let go.

"We should probably clean up," I said, trying to turn the page. "The moms...."

"Yes," he agreed. "Showers, too, I think."

I smiled coyly. "One shower...."

He liked that idea too.

We got in the stall together and turned the water on. Before picking up the soap I got down on my knees and took his softened penis in my mouth, sucking and licking away our juices. He hardened slightly, but not much, but he smiled down at me approvingly.

Then we soaped each other up and down. The squeaky cleanness was such a contrast to our salty, sweaty, musky state before. But it allowed me to properly admire his body, without just thinking of sex. And I liked the slippery silky feel of his hands across my wet skin.

When we got out of the shower we stood dripping, naked, looking at our reflections in the mirror. Me naked beside a boy – I could barely believe it. A boy I had made love to.

Both of us smiled at our reflections, revealing our wired teeth. What an absurd sight! And what a perfect one.

"I guess you can take the retainers out," he said.

But I couldn't bring myself to do it yet, grabbing the towels and beginning to dry us off. My tongue against the acrylic, the retainers were the one thing I could cling to, the one holdover that wasn't lost in the moment, and our impending separation.

We got dressed again, and cleaned away the most obvious traces of our excesses. I was definitely going to have to find some time when Mom wasn't home to wash my sheets, or I would have a lot of explaining to do....

Only then did I regretfully take out my retainers.

Now everything was back to normal. Even though everything had changed.

We were both a bit subdued. Trying not to think about how over this was. That we likely wouldn't see each other again. Not for years. Was he relieved? He didn't look it. But we both looked so spent and exhausted it was hard to read any emotion into our expressions.

We decompressed. We had some food. We tried to act *normal*. But what was normal after what we had done? My body moved in autopilot, but my mind was still racing.

Overheated from what had happened to me. It had been impossible to even begin to process it in the moment. I wondered how long it would take for it all to really sink in.

8.

I was amazed that we managed to revert to typical teen appearance by the time the moms got back. Charles was on the deck, playing on his iPad. I was pretending to start figuring out my fall and school wardrobe.

I was sure we looked guilty when the moms greeted us, but at our age we probably always look – and are – guilty of something, so maybe they couldn't tell. And it helped that Charles and his mom were under some time pressure to pack up and head to the airport, so everybody was preoccupied with that.

It was hard saying goodbye because I couldn't really say it. I couldn't say all the things I wanted to. Which maybe was better, because I really still didn't have the words. What a rollercoaster of emotions! But Charles tried to play it cool too. And it was probably good that that led to an awkward sort of goodbye hug – exactly what the moms would expect from two teens who had been forced to spend a weekend together, and anything but what they'd expect from two teens who had been fucking just a few hours earlier....

I dreaded Mom's "So did you have a good time with Charles?" question after they left.

I rolled my eyes and shrugged and hoped I wasn't too obvious about trying to avoid answering in any detail. "Yeah, he turned out to be pretty cool," I said, desperately hoping my voice wouldn't crack. "I couldn't get used to the braces," I added, "but otherwise it was fine."

"Well, thank you for your hospitality," Mom said. "Taking you away from your friends and everything. I'm sure he appreciated it. April too."

I shrugged again. "It was fine," I told her – in that voice that implied it had been an enormous sacrifice.

If she only knew.

Epilogue

I thought about Charles when I put my retainers in as I got ready for bed. He was probably still flying at 30,000 feet at that moment.

Of course, I had spent most of the evening and night thinking about Charles, and his braces, and what we had done. With the retainers in my mouth I could think of nothing else but them and him and us.

Part of me was amazed how I had dared to go along with it. Letting him take my virginity. Letting him tie me up! And everything else. Part of me wanted to be angry and resent how he had forced himself on me and sodomized me – and part of me was grateful that he had, even though I still had very mixed feelings about that unexpected violation.

I was sore, and tender. Above all I was happy. So much about sex was still mystifying and intimidating, but it was a relief to know just how pleasurable it could be and that I could partake in these joys. That it could feel natural and right. And unnatural and right! Except now I had to wonder whether any other man could ever pleasure me as intensely and perfectly as Charles had....

Charles was gone. So distant that he wasn't real any more. I knew I had to let him and everything except my memories of our time together go. Maybe I could hope that when school started I'd find a boy who could come to fill his shoes. But it was OK if that took a while. I could live off these memories for the time being. Let them sink in. There was time enough until the next such adventure. And until then I had my retainers....

I picked up my book but couldn't focus on the words. There was something else and more I wanted. I had been thinking about it a lot. The night before already, but redoubled now. Now it seemed an almost essential step.

I got out of bed and went downstairs, where Mom was still working.

"Hey, Mom?" I interrupted her.

She was surprised to see me. I didn't usually come down in my PJs after heading off to bed. But she smiled happily. "What's up, Caroline?"

"You know how I haven't been back to the orthodontist since like a few months after she said I only had to wear the retainers at night?"

Mom nodded, then squinted. "You're wearing them now, aren't you?" she said, with a surprised smile.

From how they distorted by speech, that was pretty obvious....

"I haven't seen you in those forever," she said a bit sadly. More about how I looked with them than out of nostalgia. Then she added, with a bit of panic in her voice, "You have been wearing them, haven't you?" She trusted me, but she had no way of knowing.

"Always, Mom," I assured her. "Every night. Always." Which was only a slight exaggeration. But she knew and understood that there were impossible nights – like sleepovers – when I couldn't.

She looked relieved. "So you were saying?"

"Could you make me an appointment with the orthodontist? Just to check everything really is like it should be."

"Charles and his braces got you spooked?" she smiled. "Did he really get braces again because he didn't wear his retainers like he was supposed to?"

"Pretty much. But it's a little more complicated, I think. Anyway, I want to make sure about mine." I took a deep breath. "I think maybe, since I only wear them at night, I need more substantial ones. You know, that hold more, better...."

Mom nodded. She didn't really understand, but she understood that maybe I was worried. After seeing Charles, who wouldn't be? "I'm sure they're fine, if you're wearing them like you're supposed to."

"But I'd really like to get the orthodontist to confirm that everything is exactly right."

"Of course," Mom agreed. "That sounds like a good idea. I'll make an appointment first thing in the morning. Just as long she doesn't say we need to put you back in braces...."

I smiled. I knew it wouldn't come to *that*.

I couldn't help but notice how Mom's expression changed as with my smile I fully revealed the two silvery retainer wires. How she pitied me for having those running across my teeth. No wonder I never wore them around her.

"Thanks, Mom," I said, unable to hide my joy and relief, at getting this out in the open and taking this step. I even hugged her, which surprised her. She must have figured Charles's fate had really put a horrible scare into me.

I turned to go back to my room, but then remembered the other important thing. "When you make the appointment...could you ask them to put me in the back room? The one with the door, all the way in the back?"

Mom looked slightly taken aback. The bad memories probably flooded back. Her being led back there, the door opened, revealing me, strapped in the chair and with my newly braced mouth gaping at her, held wide open by the cheek retractor.... "Isn't that where they put the braces on you?" she said, her voice cracking slightly.

I blushed. She remembered exactly. But I had my excuse lined up. I nodded. "Yeah. But it's private, right? And I'm kind of embarrassed about these," I said, pointing at the retainers. Mom nodded. Of course. *That* she understood.

"I really don't want anyone there to see me with them," I explained. "The other kids. I don't want to seem like a patient. And that's the only room that's like really sealed off."

"Of course, dear. I'll ask."

"No, please! Make sure! Even if they say it would be private in one of the other rooms too, I really want to be sure, and that's the only room with a door. The other stuff about it...that doesn't matter. OK?"

Mom smiled, but I knew she understood that if I was this insistent that it was important to me, and she'd make it happen.

"OK, Caroline. Total privacy!"

I beamed again – and she tried not to grimace at the sight of the retainers again. I would have given her a goodnight, thank-you kiss on the cheek, but from how she pulled her head just slightly back we both knew she didn't want that. Not while I was wearing these.

I skipped lightly to my room and bed. A small burden lifted, an opportunity grabbed. I wasn't exactly sure what I was hoping for, or that I could explain it to the orthodontist, but I hoped that when I was strapped down in the chair I would be able to make myself clear.

I did want – I needed! – something more substantial. A bigger retainer. Mouth-filling even, more or less. Something whose presence I couldn't overlook or ignore. That was so *there*. And maybe even with a headgear to help hold it in place and mouth...?

I hoped the orthodontist would understand. But she was an orthodontist, a braces expert. She had to know, and understand. I couldn't be the only patient who came to such realizations. I needed this. I'd have to work up the nerve to make my demand clear – but it mattered enough to me that I was confident I could. It meant everything to me.

Turning out the lights, still smelling Charles's and my smells on my pillow and sheets, the smooth surfaces of the retainers against my tongue a reminder and comfort, I twisted achingly in bed. My ligaments and muscles were pleasantly sore, like after a long day spent playing sports. My crotch was sore well into me, front and back, but even that was an agreeable sensation, spreading a tingling warmth that reminded me of what I had accomplished, and what had been accomplished with me.

I was happy, and I drifted off to sleep happy, the sparkle of Charles's braces, and the memory of their feel against my lips and breasts the last impressions in my mind as I fell into a deep, perfect slumber.

—THE END—

About the author

Catherine Aimes was born and grew up in Michigan. She now lives in England with her husband and their two daughters, who both went through having braces.

Catherine Aimes can be reached at:

    info@intraoralpress.com

Other books from Intraoral Press

Brooke in Braces (by Cathy Aimes)

Our other Dr.Samantha Wrighting books:

Retainer Girl
Love and Braces
The Braced Experience
A Bracing Life: The Dr. Samantha Wrighting Interview
Bracing Daydreams
Braced in Wedlock
Braces and Beyond
Mothers, Daughters, Braces

Our Dr.Samantha Wrighting shorts:

Headgeared
Madison's Braces
Lights, Camera, Braces!

Our Erotic Orthodontic Encounter books:

Notwithstanding Braces
The Braced Tease
Bracing Times with Cecilia
Living the Braced Fantasy

For additional information

Visit our website at:
www.intraoralpress.com

Braced for Seduction is the fifth Erotic Orthodontic Encounter novel from Intraoral Press.

Visit our website for all the latest information about author Catherine Aimes, and the complete line of Dr. Samantha Wrighting and Intraoral Press novels.

*Look for new novels
from the Offices of Dr. Samantha Wrighting*

Printed in Great Britain
by Amazon